THE MOSAIC MURDER

The artists' reception at the Mosaic Gallery in Tucson, Arizona is a success. However, next day, the body of Armando, the owner's husband, is discovered. Every artist is a suspect, with his or her own reasons to want him out of the picture. And who stole the sculpture of the goddess Gaia? Detective Maggie Reardon investigates, but with her disastrous personal life and being viciously attacked in her home, can she survive long enough to find the culprit . . . ?

LONNI LEES

THE MOSAIC MURDER

Complete and Unabridged

LINFORD
Leicester

First published in Great Britain

First Linford Edition
published 2013

A catalogue record for this book is available
from the British Library.

ISBN 978–1–4448–1546–7

Published by
F. A. Thorpe (Publishing)
Anstey, Leicestershire

Set by Words & Graphics Ltd.
Anstey, Leicestershire
Printed and bound in Great Britain by
T. J. International Ltd., Padstow, Cornwall

This book is printed on acid-free paper

1

The Burning Sky

Detective Maggie Reardon holstered her sidearm as she walked out of the locker room and into the hallway of the Tucson Arizona Police Department. Her short auburn hair spiked over her eyebrows threatening to stab her in the eyes, but trips to the beauty shop weren't on her to-do list. There were more important things and a quick snip in front of the bathroom mirror served her just fine. It was quick, it was free, and it got the job done. Self-nurturing wasn't in her vocabulary.

A fellow cop passed her as she walked down the hall, accompanied by a young rookie she hadn't seen before. He looked more like a high school kid than someone capable of protecting anyone, but looks could be deceiving. They could actually work to one's advantage, giving an unexpected edge. The rookie gave her a double-take as they passed, turned and gave her a wink. She ignored him, but as they continued their walk in the other direction she overheard the seasoned cop comment to the kid under his breath.

'Don't let that cute turned-up nose and perfect mouth fool you. That little mick stings like a scorpion,' said Jerry Montana to the rookie beside him.

'I can hear you, Jerry,' said Maggie.

Hah, you reject one person's advances and pretty soon they think they've got you pegged. She had her own rules and they served her well. No romantic involvement in the workplace, that was rule number one, especially with some married cop on the prowl like that jerk Jerry had been. At least he'd taken the hint and laid off. She gave him credit for that much, even if he had said some unkind things about her around the locker room. They were worse than teenagers. Well, let them think what they want. Life was complicated enough.

She spat on her hand and shoved the unruly red spikes from her eyes as she exited the door and walked across the parking lot.

It was going to be another triple digit day.

Maggie walked across the blistering pavement, opened the door to her squad car and slid in. The steering wheel was hot beneath her fingers and she took a deep breath. She wasn't much for introspection, but it had been two years since her husband divorced her and two weeks since her last boyfriend, Marty, had yelled 'uncle.' A part of her was relieved, but she still wondered how much of it was her own doing. She pushed the thought away. It was easier to focus on her job. And more satisfying. Maybe that was part of the problem. Her job came first and the men in her life came in second. A really bad second. If she wasn't going to pamper herself she certainly wasn't going to pamper some man. She wouldn't baby-sit nor would she morph into the image of what they thought she should to be. If they didn't get it, then they didn't get it. And there were warning signs with her latest ex. Alarms rang that she'd refused to hear. Had she really been that desperate? Enough thinking on that subject, she thought with a dismissive shrug. Some people were meant to fly solo. She turned the key in the ignition, revved the engine, threw it into gear and edged her way into the traffic on South Stone Avenue.

Even in this heat things didn't slow down. You'd think people would be too tired to raise hell, but the escalating temperatures just shortened their tempers and quickened the speed of their trigger fingers. It didn't take much to set them off, and with luck it just ended with a domestic disturbance call or a black eye and some bruises. Sometimes it ended with a dead body and a free ride to jail.

The health nuts still rode their bikes up Gates Pass, slowing to a crawl the cars unable to pass them along the narrow road, oblivious to their surroundings and the honking horns. Hikers still challenged the burning desert, occasionally falling off a cliff or getting bitten by a rattler or stumbling over the corpse of an illegal. Sometimes one of those corpses might have a tell-tale bullet hole, but usually they just died of heat and exhaustion. Instead of reaching the promised land they ended up in the morgue, unclaimed and unidentified.

★   ★   ★

Tall saguaro cacti stood like sentinels, arms reaching upward and outward, as if their prickly appendages protected their domain from the sun, the solitude, and the passage of time. The floor of the Arizona-Sonoran desert cringed under the late June blistering heat. Its surface wore a myriad of cracks like the skin of an old Mexican woman, ravaged by time and indifference. As the late afternoon temperature rose to 108 degrees, lizards hid under rocks, snakes found refuge in stolen burrows, all was silent save for the whoosh and flap of vultures and hawks whose keen eyes scavenged the unforgiving landscape below for a scurrying rabbit or rodent. The desert was a brutal place that held little mercy, but the tough adapted, survived, and even flourished.

Like the mythical phoenix rising from the ashes, come spring plants would flower and mesquite trees bloom, as would the blue palo verde trees before dropping their edible beans to the dry earth. If one took the time to stop and look, they would see that what, on the surface, appeared to be a long-forgotten graveyard teemed with life and promise.

In the distance, the tall buildings of Tucson rose toward a smoke-filled sky. The ash from distant wild fires floated across the landscape, hiding the outline of the Catalina Mountains to the north and the Rincon Mountains to the east and covering the landscape like a dirty blanket of Los Angeles smog. The wind to the south stirred and spread the flames, devouring miles of brush and any buildings that stood in its path. Prayers for the welcome rains of the summer monsoon went unanswered.

The Mosaic Gallery nestled among old Victorian houses and ramshackle commercial buildings in the heart of Tucson. The large, arched adobe entry that led to the gallery was a virtual canvas of tiles, some handmade by local artists, imbedded alongside shards of broken glass and ceramic and shiny little fragments of shattered dishes. The tiled archway was a group effort, anyone adding a found piece or two as the mood struck them. The result was both chaotic and beautiful. A woman in her forties squatted at the arch like a bullfrog, a small bucket of broken tiles at her side. One by one, she pressed them into the wet plaster with blistered hands. She wiped the perspiration from her face with the back of her arm and exhaled a disgruntled sigh. Adrian Velikson was a short woman, barely 5′ 2″, and nearly as wide as she was tall. She was masculine and sturdy and wore a determined scowl and a buzz-cut.

Beyond the archway a cobbled walkway led to the building, crowned in Spanish tile, with a second-story addition at the rear with a separate entrance to its private quarters. To the right of the walkway was a small area where two people stood holding their rakes, shaded from the scorching late afternoon sun by two gnarled mesquite trees. Rocco La Crosse cursed under his breath as he raked another huge pile of tiny leaves and lifted them into the trash barrel.

'I swear, these things never stop dropping,' he complained as he raked around a large metal sculpture. 'Those trees shed worse than a Dalmatian dog.' He raked around the foot of a statue that stood as tall as a full-grown man, a welded hodgepodge of found metal, ranging from car parts to plumbing fixtures to an old metal bicycle wheel that served as its face. The sculpture was his handiwork, as hard and rough looking as Rocco himself. He was a large man, bulky arms tattooed from fingertips to shoulder, exposed by his wife beater sleeveless tee. A scruffy dark beard nearly hid his gentle smile while bushy eyebrows framed his twinkling eyes. His potbelly was hard as granite and jutted over the leather tooled belt that held up his jeans. A silver earring dangled from one ear. His dark hair was pulled back into a ponytail at the nape of his neck, damp from perspiration and matted with dust.

'We're almost done,' said Barbara

Atwell. 'It has to look good for tonight's reception.'

Trying to keep pace with Rocco was wearing her out, but this was her gallery and her responsibility. This was her life. She was thankful for the volunteers and artists who helped her keep things in order but she worked as hard or harder than all of them combined. Barbara stood a statuesque 5′ 9″, and carried herself with the grace of a runway model. Her legs were long and her lean body was crowned with silky blonde, shoulder length hair. High cheekbones accentuated her straight nose and determined mouth and her natural beauty belied the fact that she was at the high end of her forties. Nature and genetics had been good to her.

Barbara leaned against her rake and sighed, then continued raking the tiny leaves into piles and lifting them into the trash can.

'Okay,' she said. 'This will have to be good enough.'

'Fine by me,' said Rocco. He wiped the gritty perspiration from his brow and threw his rake to the ground, looking around for any loose twigs they may have missed. It was an exercise in futility. By tomorrow morning hundreds more mesquite leaves would have fallen to replace those picked up today.

'Adrian,' Barbara said. 'It's getting late, could you wind it up there?'

'Hey, I'm on a roll here,' said Adrian as she lifted another broken shard from the bucket. 'Three more tiles, just three more.'

'Right. And then three more after that.'

Rocco picked up the rakes and leaned them against the side of the building, then dragged the trashcan beside them. He looked around and decided it was a job well done. He could feel the tension building between Adrian and Barbara, thickening like bad gravy in the hot air. He didn't like tension or arguing or anything that edged its way in to disturb his inner calm. Whenever those things threatened to raise their ugly heads Rocco was the peacemaker, the one to smooth over hurt feelings and imagined slights and ease things back into his comfort zone.

'C'mon, Adrian,' he said. 'We've got to get a move on.'

'Don't bug me.'

'Put it away and I'll give you a ride home,' he offered. He gave her a disapproving frown, with a nearly imperceptible shake of his head meant only for her eyes. She caught it and gave him a nod.

'Gotcha,' she said.

Barbara looked at her watch and exhaled an impatient sigh. It was getting late and there was still no sign of her husband. She cleared her throat, then spoke: 'I'm sorry guys, but could you stop by The Trader's on the way and pick up some food for the reception? I'd really appreciate it.'

Adrian pulled herself up from where she was squatting with a loud grunt and reached for the bucket of tiles.

'Isn't that *Arrrrmando's* job?' she said with a sarcastic roll of the *r* in Armando.

Barbara looked at her apologetically. 'He hasn't made it back from Nogales yet. I guess he got tied up at the border check again.'

'He's always got some excuse,' Adrian said. Then muttered under her breath, 'Gullible.'

Rocco walked over to where Adrian stood and put his arm around her broad shoulders. 'Just let it go,' he whispered to her, in another attempt to diffuse the tension that mixed with the hot afternoon heat. 'You know you're just spitting in the wind, let it go.'

She ignored him and went on. 'Picking up more of those Mexican artifact rip-offs from across the border? He had to do it today? My God Barbara, how can you display that crap in the gallery? It's . . . '

'It sells.'

'At what cost to your reputation? They're worthless tchotchkes that belong in a ninety-nine cent store. I'm sorry, but I just don't get it.'

'It sells,' Barbara repeated.

'Okay ladies, enough,' said Rocco. 'We'll gladly pick up the food, Barbara, won't we Adrian?'

'Nice to know how valuable we are when you need something,' Adrian muttered under her breath.

Rocco shook his head and gave her another disapproving scowl. 'I'll get you a six-pack of those orange-cranberry scones, sweetness,' he said.

Barbara went inside the gallery and returned with some petty cash. She handed it to Rocco and thanked him. He kissed her on the cheek, took Adrian by the arm and led her out to his parked van.

'Where's your Victory?' she asked.

'Motorcycle's in the shop,' he said, opening the door to the van for her, hinges creaking. 'It's getting gatlin' gun exhaust tips.'

'You should spoil your women as much as you spoil that bike,' she said as she slid into the passenger seat.

'If I could find one as charming as you I would,' he said with a wink.

'Why Rocco, you keep up that flattery and I might be tempted to go straight.'

'That'll be the day,' he said with a hearty laugh.

★　★　★

13

Detective Maggie Reardon pulled the squad car into an empty space in front of the mini-mart. The heat was stifling and she wanted a cold drink. The day had been reasonably quiet and she felt more relaxed than she had in days. She turned off the key and slid out, feet touching the hot pavement as she slammed the car door and walked to the entrance. The leather from her gun belt squeaked in unison with her steps as she pushed her way inside. The bell above the door jingled, announcing her arrival.

Carlos, a slightly-built elderly man, looked up from where he stood behind the counter by the cash register and gave her a smile. His yellow-toothed grin filled half his face and made his dark eyes sparkle. '*Buenos días, Señorita* Maggie,' he said. 'You be out catching the bad boys, si?'

Maggie gave him a wink and a nod, then headed for the back of the store by the fountain drinks. She pulled out a cup, placed it under the spigot, and began filling it with ice and soda. She was the only customer in the store, so decided she'd take a few minutes to chat with Carlos before heading back out. He was a kindly old soul and had been a permanent fixture by the cash register for as long as she could remember. He was there when she was a little girl who would come in for a bag of chips after school. He was the one who firmly told her no when she walked in as a teenager trying to buy her first pack of cigarettes. He consoled her when her parents died. And he was there to congratulate her when she walked in wearing her uniform for the first time, pride filling his eyes. Carlos was a second father to her, always knowing the right words to make her feel better when something in her life went haywire and always there to praise her when praise was due.

After Maggie pressed the lid in place and shoved in a straw, she walked down the candy aisle in search of the sugar fix that would serve as today's lunch. Not a good balance of the basic food groups, especially with a day that always began with four cups of black coffee and five cigarettes, but it would do. At least, she

15

thought, I usually pick up a Mickey D or something during the day to get my protein and vegetables. She knelt down to check out the array of candy bars lined up along the bottom row of the aisle.

The bell over the door jangled as a customer walked in and headed for the cold beer in the refrigerator case along the side wall. He was a wiry little guy, not much more than a teenager, with acned skin and a nervous twitch. He pulled out a six-pack, closed the refrigerator door with his skinny butt, did a quick look around the store and headed for the register. He plopped down the beer with a thud.

'I have to see some identification, please sir,' said Carlos, eying him.

'Ain't got none,' said the kid.

'I'm sorry, *señor*, but it's the law,' Carlos shrugged.

'Okay, okay,' said the kid as he reached into his pocket and pulled out a gun, aiming it at Carlos with a shaky hand. 'Here's my identification, now open up the register and give me what you've got.'

'Please, *no problema, señor*,' said

Carlos, holding out his palms in a gesture of defeat.

'Hurry up.'

Carlos opened the cash drawer, reached in, and filled his hands with bills. He held the money out, offering it to the skinny thug who held the gun.

'I oughta shoot you for giving me a hard time, old man,' he said as he grabbed the cash with one hand and began shoving it in his pocket. 'It'd serve you right.'

The kid heard the click at the same instant he felt the gun shoved into his back.

'It might be a good idea to drop that gun,' Maggie said from where she stood behind him. 'And I mean right now, not next week. Drop it. Slowly.'

The kid lowered him arm and placed the gun on the counter in front of Carlos. Then he spun around in an attempt to disarm his unknown assailant. Before he finished spinning he was hit with a knee in the groin that brought him to his knees. He groaned. Then a foot shoved him forward onto the floor and he felt someone's full weight pressing into his back.

'Put your hands behind your back. Now.'

His head was spinning. Robbing the store seemed like a no-brainer yesterday when he'd come in and seen the old man alone behind the counter. All he had to do was wave a gun and it would be a done deal and he'd have enough money to pay his rent. Maybe even buy a little crack. But now, as he put his hands behind his back and heard the unwelcome click of the cold handcuffs as they wrapped around his wrists and secured him, he got a reality check. Things don't always go as planned. Especially if you make plans when you're stoned.

'Stand up, punk,' Maggie said as she hoisted him to his feet and gave him a shove forward in the direction of the glass doors. She stopped and motioned to Carlos, who was still holding his breath, eyes wide.

'Come on over here, Carlos.'

He walked around the counter to where Maggie stood holding the kid, who was starting to squirm uncomfortably against her hold.

'I think he's got something in his pocket that belongs to you,' she said. 'Let's make life simple here, okay? Just reach in and take what belongs to you. We can fill out the report later. Hey, it might give us a chance for a more relaxed visit, right?'

Carlos hesitated, then cautiously stepped forward and reached into the pocket to retrieve his hard earned cash.

'*Gracias, Señorita* Maggie,' he said. '*Muchas gracias.*'

'All in a days work, *papacita*,' she said, giving the kid a shove against the front door as Carlos counted out his money and put it back into the cash drawer. He slammed it shut with a sigh of relief.

Then he noticed the gun where it still lay on the counter.

'Do not forget your evidence,' he smiled, picking it up and walking over to Maggie.

'Thanks.' Maggie had her hands full with the punk and thought for a second. 'Just shove it into my pocket, okay?'

'*Sí, sí,*' he said. Holding the gun with two fingers as if it were a live rattlesnake about to strike he walked over to them, then quickly shoved it into her pocket and took three steps backwards. The kid strained his neck to get his first good look at the person holding him captive.

'You gotta be kidding me,' he said as he locked eyes with her. 'You ain't nothin' but a skanky little *puta*!' He let out a few expletives and a nervous, high pitched laugh.

'You tried me once, punk. Are you really dumb enough to try me again?'

'I could take you if I didn't have these cuffs on.'

'Like you did before?'

'Hey, you caught me by surprise, that's all.'

'Ain't life full of little surprises though? You want to try me before or after you wet your pants?'

Carlos took a few more steps backwards and when he felt he was at a safe enough distance he chimed in his two cents worth.

'Did no anybody ever teach you it eez

no nice to point guns at people?' he said.

The kid looked back at him and said, 'Like I guess I musta dropped the book and lost the lesson, old man.'

Carlos watched with pride as Maggie hauled the kid through the door and out to the squad car. She be something else, my miss Maggie, he thought with a smile. Like a little firecracker. As she shoved him in the back seat, Carlos could hear her say:

'You know, you really ought to practice some impulse control. It could keep you out of a heap of trouble.'

2

A Rowdy Reception

Barbara Atwell walked through the empty gallery, dust cloth in hand. She ran the cloth across the top of the frames that held the artwork and across the surfaces of the table tops. Everything had to look perfect. She put down the dust cloth and picked up the spray bottle of glass cleaner and paper towels and began to clean the glass fronts that displayed the hand made Paloma Blanca jewelry. The gallery was her life. A dream realized with sweat equity, intelligence and the ability to choose art that the public loved. The recession had put a dent in things but she still managed to keep afloat by mixing more affordable pieces with the more costly ones. It was true, she had to lower her standards a bit, but it kept Mosaic in the black. Ten inexpensive items were an easier sell in this economy than one pricey one. Hard times necessitated hard choices. She had seen too many pricey, trendy galleries go under in the last year and was determined not to become another fatality. She'd worked too hard and long to lose it now and would do whatever was necessary to keep afloat.

The back door creaked open on its unoiled hinges, then closed with a bang, causing Barbara to jump.

'Armando? Is that you?'

'I am so sorry, my love,' he said as he entered the room. 'The traffic,' he said in explanation in his soft south of the border accent. Armando stood there with a smile, white teeth glistening against flawless olive skin, dark mischievous eyes twinkling under thick lashes as he looked at his wife. He was in his mid-twenties, in contrast to her forties, and every time she looked at him her heart melted like some love struck kid. She couldn't help it. He stood before her, tall and perfect, looking like some burnished Aztec god.

And he knew it.

'No excuses necessary,' she said, setting down the glass cleaner and walking over to him. She put her arms around him and held his body close. 'I missed you,' she whispered.

'And I you, my love.'

He kissed her. Every kiss made this otherwise strong and independent woman weak in the knees. There were times she wanted to kick herself or give herself a hard slap across the face to snap back to reality. But he affected her like a forbidden drug and she had no intention of kicking the habit. Armando was the only man who ever won her over. The others had been a pleasant diversion, but handsome Armando had totally mesmerized her with his Latin charm. Despite the age difference and the unwelcome advice and warnings from well-meaning friends, when he proposed she'd said yes with no hesitation. The wedding was simple, a small ceremony performed by a shaman right at the gallery, surrounded by artists and close friends. Local drummers performed the wedding march while tribal dancers twirled and scattered flower petals along the path.

It was perfect.

After the ceremony, Armando moved into Barbara's living quarters above the gallery. Their life together was good. And as non-traditional as Barbara herself.

'Should we go upstairs?' she asked him.

Armando pulled away from her and smiled. 'I am so tired from the trip, my sweet. I just need to shower and take a little siesta. Perhaps tomorrow?'

Barbara pouted and turned away from him.

'Tomorrow,' he said. 'The day will belong to the two of us and we will never leave the bedroom.' He pulled her back to him. '*Mañana* will be *romantico*.'

'*Sí, mañana.*' She started to hum the old Peggy Lee song as she returned to her cleaning. '*Mañana* is good enough for me.'

★ ★ ★

Maggie Reardon slammed the door of her small adobe, the same house in which she'd been raised. She'd booked the kid, gone back to visit with her friend Carlos, and filled out the necessary paperwork.

25

Now the punk was somebody else's problem and it was time to relax. She unbuckled her gun belt, placed it on the side table and collapsed into the over-stuffed chair her father had sat in as far back as she could remember. She missed him. She missed them both. Her overweight black cat jumped onto her lap, meowing impatiently for his dinner. She pushed him off and onto the floor, where he sat glaring at her.

'Just hold on there, Prowler,' she said to him. 'Your turn's coming.'

As she was pulling off her shoes the phone rang. She tossed a shoe onto the floor, barely missing the cat, who puffed up his fur in protest but didn't budge. She debated not answering. All she wanted was an Irish whiskey and a relaxed smoke. But the ringing wouldn't stop. She reached across to the phone on the side table and as she picked up the receiver she removed the second shoe with her other hand and dropped it to the floor. It hit the tiles with a thud. Prowler voiced his disapproval with a low growl, but refused to move even an inch out of the path of her missiles.

'What,' she said into the phone, impatience and exhaustion in her voice.

It was Marty, her latest ex-boyfriend.

'We really need to talk, Maggie,' he said.

'We did talk, remember?'

'But I miss you.' The same annoying whine was in his voice, the sound of a child determined to get his way.

She said nothing. His voice grated on her and made her bristle. But it also conjured images of his wavy blonde hair and sky blue eyes and the smell of his cologne and the feel of his touch. She found herself weighing the pros and cons of their relationship just as she had weeks before. The right decision was made, even if he had been the instigator. It was a done deal.

'Talk to me, baby. Please. We can work this out.'

'We did work it out.'

'You *know* it was a mistake. You've gotta miss me as much as I miss you.'

'No, I don't *gotta*. It was best for us both. You know that, Marty.'

27

Maggie only half listened as Marty stated his well rehearsed argument. He told her how good they were together. Good for who, exactly? Somewhere during his monologue she interjected something about him needing a mother rather than a lover, but her truthful gem either went over his head or he'd chosen to ignore it.

'Marty, we were good in bed, that's all,' she interrupted. It had taken her a while to figure out that a man could be a great lover but not be good for much else. Initially, all those flying hormones had fogged her judgment, but when all was said and done, being proficient in the bedroom didn't produce enough glue to hold the rest of the relationship together. So sad, so true.

He droned on, making point after weak point, until she reached the end of her patience.

'I'm tired,' she said and hung up.

When the phone rang again Maggie Reardon ignored it. Instead of answering she walked into the kitchen, Prowler at her heels, and opened a can of cat food.

That was about all the nurturing she had the stomach for.

★   ★   ★

Barbara Atwell turned on the window air conditioning units in the gallery's three public rooms on her way to unlock the front door. She flipped on the exterior lights and set ashtrays on the porch for the smokers. The artist's reception was a half hour away and things still had to be put in order. Some days she was overwhelmed and today was no exception. Armando hadn't come downstairs yet to set up bottles of Chianti and champagne for the bar. The folding table was waiting for food, but Rocco and Adrian hadn't yet arrived with bags from The Trader's. Barbara placed paper plates and plastic forks on the table, along with napkins, then stacked cocktail napkins at the bar alongside plastic cups. Beads of perspiration gathered above her top lip and impatience knotted her stomach. Where was help when she needed it? It had eased slightly, but the day's heat promised a warm night magnified by a room filled with people. The air conditioners churned out what coolness they could, but upgrading wasn't in the budget.

She was ready to snap.

Wine bottles in hand, Armando entered the room. He walked across the floor and put the champagne in the mini-fridge behind the counter and placed two bottles of Chianti on the bar. He turned and gave Barbara a well-practiced apologetic grin. 'That should get things started,' he said. There was no way she could get angry when he flashed that smile. He played her like a honky-tonk piano and she gladly tap danced to his tune. And oh, what a glorious dance it was.

'About time,' she said. She wanted to say more, maybe scold him a little, but his presence calmed her mood and helped her relax. She let it go. They were holding hands like honeymooners when Rocco and Adrian came through the front door, laden with grocery bags and giggling at some off-color joke.

'Oh, you can be so naughty,' Adrian laughed, her stocky body shaking so hard she almost dropped one of the bags.

'That's why you love me, baby.'

'Permit me to help, *mi amiga.*' Armando said as he rushed over to Adrian, freeing a bag from her grasp.

'*Gracias*, but I'm not your *amiga.*' Then she added: 'You sure know how to shovel it, don't you Arrr-mando?'

'Ah, *mi amiga es inteligente* as well as *bonita*,' he said with a flash of his white teeth, returning the sarcasm. Even when he's being nasty he can't help flirting, Adrian thought to herself as he gave her his best dimpled smile. He was probably born flirting with the midwife who delivered him. He was incurable, a real piece of work.

The three of them walked over to the table and began emptying the bags, putting cheese squares in one dish and assorted snacks in the rest. It took less than five minutes and everything was in order and ready for the reception. Adrian and Rocco ignored Barbara's sideways glances as they worked. At least her dark mood had lifted somewhat since Armando's return from Nogales.

Rocco clapped his hands together and addressing Barbara said: 'Anything else?'

'Just thank you. I appreciate all you do to help around here. You too, Adrian.'

Adrian gave her a half-smile, sadness in her eyes as she looked at her friend. Barbara was wearing a long, teal blue dress and high heels that added three more inches to her already statuesque height. Her blonde hair caressed her shoulders and touched the blue sapphires she wore around her long neck. She was exquisite. But she was Armando's. For the most part anyway.

Rocco turned at the sound of loud banging and headed towards the door.

'My god, don't they know it's unlocked?' Barbara said.

Rocco opened the door just as Belinda Blume, facing away from him, prepared to give it one more kick with the sole of her shoe. In her hands she held her heavy contribution to the show. Frizzy light brown hair fell in her face as she turned at the sound of the door opening and lowered her foot to the ground.

'Darn near gotcha,' she said. 'Thanks. I was afraid I'd drop it.'

She walked inside to where Adrian, Barbara and Armando stood talking. 'Hi all,' she said. 'Barb, baby doll, where do you want this?'

Barbara pointed to a pedestal sandwiched between Armando's shelf and the display case that held the Paloma Blanca jewelry. Belinda was tempted to say something about not wanting her beautiful sculpture next to Armando's knickknacks, but being next to his crap actually made her piece look all the better. With calloused hands, he placed her artwork on the pedestal then stood back, looking at it with admiration.

'I topped myself,' she said.

Adrian walked over to take a closer look.

'It's magical,' she said. 'Gaia! It's the goddess.' She reached out and felt its soft, round stomach bursting with child, then lifted it. 'Heavy,' she said as she carefully placed it back down with a grunt. Gaia was formed from red clay, sitting proud in all her nakedness, a wreath of flowers meticulously carved into her tangled hair. Adrian thought how much the piece resembled the artist. Full-bodied, short necked, thick fingered. 'She's a masterpiece, Belinda.'

'Oh Goddess,' Barbara chanted, 'source of gods and mortals, all-fertile, all-destroying Gaia!' Then added: 'You've captured her essence to perfection, Belinda. You should be proud.'

'First in my prayer, before all deities, I call upon Gaia, primeval prophetess, the Greek great earth mother,' chimed in Adrian with a dramatic bow.

'Oy, enough already,' said Belinda, grinning ear to ear. 'Hey, Armando, *bubeleh*, how about uncorking some of that bubbly? I'm ready to rock and roll.'

'Make that two,' said Adrian.

'Three,' said Rocco.

'Three's an unlucky number,' said Barbara. 'Better make that four.'

'And one for the bartender,' said Armando, as he popped the cork and began to pour.

The bell above the door jingled as

Misty Waters entered the gallery. She walked softly through the first public room, pleased that her oils were displayed where they were the first thing one's eyes set sight on upon entering. Her paintings were large and abstract, in shades of white as pale as her own complexion. Despite being only thirty her head was crowned with snow white hair. As always, Misty dressed in flowing white gauze from head to toe. She was as abstract as her art and as difficult to figure. She floated in like a passing cloud, avoiding eye contact.

'Misty, I'm so glad you could come,' said Barbara. 'I can always depend on you.'

Rocco walked over to where Misty stood. She recoiled from his welcoming hug, her arms remaining awkwardly at her sides. Physical contact clearly made her uncomfortable. He pulled away and said, 'Why don't I get you something to drink? What would you like?'

'Do we have white wine?' she asked.

Rocco turned to Armando with a slight smile. He should have guessed that Misty Waters would only drink something white. Everything about her was white. Weird, he thought with a shrug. White as an unpainted wall, a blank canvas, an icy snowbank. How, he wondered, did she manage to stay so pale in the Arizona sun? She was spooky, like a vampire who only ventured out after sundown. In their close-knit gallery family Misty was their resident enigma.

Armando fished through the mini-fridge and took out a bottle of white zinfandel. 'Will this work for the fine *señorita*?' She nodded her approval. He poured some into a plastic cup and handed it to Rocco who in turn handed it to Misty.

'Thank you,' she whispered as she turned and walked into another room, looking at the display of art on the walls, ignoring everyone as she faded silently into the background.

'Talk about distant,' Adrian said under her breath.

Barbara walked over to where Adrian stood. 'But she always comes to the receptions. That's more than some of the artists do.'

'She never stays long. It's like an obligation that she has to suffer through.'

Rocco joined the two women. 'Remember, we're a family. We don't judge, we accept. Where would we be if we didn't embrace one another just the way we are? Not one of us is perfect. And some of us are flawed almost beyond repair.' He laughed at his own comment. 'That's what makes us special, don't you think?'

'You're painfully magnanimous,' said Adrian. 'She's so invisible she could be a hit man or a spy for the CIA. Or a serial killer. They say it's the quiet ones you've got to look out for.'

'We can all learn a thing or two from you Rocco,' said Barbara. 'You're a highly evolved soul and I truly believe the gods brought you here to guide us. You're my favorite motorcycle riding, rough and tumble, tattooed guru.'

'Aw shucks, ma'am,' he said in his best cowboy drawl.

'Mary Rose,' said Adrian as the elderly

woman walked in. She wore a floral dress and a soft lavender silk shawl that reflected the color of the flower in her hair. 'I'm so glad you came. You're beautiful as always.'

'For a crone, my dear, for a crone.'

Armando walked out from where he stood at the bar and took Mary Rose's hand, her skin as thin and frail as crêpe paper. He twirled her around gracefully. 'You, my lady, are my favorite work of art.'

'Enough with your flattery, you silly rascal. How about pouring me a glass of cold bubbles?' Mary Rose walked over to a chair and sat down while Barbara filled a small dish with cheese and crackers and grapes and took them to her, along with the glass of champagne that Armando had poured.

'Your watercolors look beautiful,' Barbara said. 'I would wager every one is going to sell.'

'That'd be a plus,' she said, looking over to Armando. 'You certainly have quite the catch there. As does he, of course. Such a handsome couple. You know if I were a bit younger I'd have his shoes under my bed in no time.'

'He does have his appeal,' Barbara answered with a laugh.

3

Shades of Yesterday

Prowler had finished his food and settled comfortably on Maggie Reardon's lap, licking his paws. She wore a ragged chenille bathrobe and had the television on low to an old rerun of *Cops* as she picked away at a tasteless TV dinner. It was worse than not eating at all and she wondered why she kept buying them. Maybe because they were fast and no fuss. Or maybe because the photographs on the package made them look downright yummy. Or maybe she thought one of these days she'd hit on one that was actually edible. She hadn't yet. Was it masochism? Hardly. Lack of imagination? More likely than not it was just plain laziness. She pushed Prowler onto the floor and set down the tray, which still held a few bites of over-salted beef trapped in congealing gravy.

'There you go, Prowler. Have at it boy.'

Prowler took one sniff and gagged as if he were ready to cough up a fur ball. He looked at the tray with disgust, then jumped back onto Maggie's lap.

'I guess you're smarter than I am,' she said scratching him behind the ear. 'Your cat food probably has more flavor. Maybe I'll try it sometime.'

Prowler began to purr, digging his sharp claws affectionately into her thigh.

'You're right. It couldn't be any worse.'

She looked up at the television just as two cops were shoving some perp into the back seat of their squad car. 'Cuff 'em and stuff 'em!' she yelled at the set. 'Way to go!'

The black cat let out a low growl in his best imitation of a Siamese.

'Makes one proud, doesn't it, Prowler?'

There was a knock at the front door. Then another. And another.

Maggie rose, tossed Prowler across her shoulder and walked to the door. She looked through the peephole and there stood Marty the ex, flowers in hand. She was in no mood to answer. He kept knocking and she kept looking through the little round hole waiting for him to give up and go away. His baby blues peeked through curly blond hair that fell forward over his eyebrows, his expression naive yet determined.

He was becoming a pest.

'Please open the door, Maggie. I know you're in there.'

He held the flowers against his chest and furrowed his brow.

'I brought a peace offering.'

She yelled at him. 'You're starting to act like a stalker, Marty. Get away from here before I call in for back-up and have you hauled away.'

It was a full minute before he turned and walked away, defeated.

'The guy is starting to creep me out,' she said to the cat.

She waited until she was certain he was gone, then slowly opened the door. On the ground, wilting from the heat, lay a small bouquet of dainty pink roses. She reached down, Prowler still draped across her shoulder, picked them up and went inside, locking and bolting the door behind her. For a split second she thought of putting them in water. Then she threw them into the wastebasket, returned to her comfortable chair and kicked up the volume on the TV.

Tickling the cat under his chin she muttered, 'He doesn't know me at all. If there's anything I'm *not*, it's dainty pink!'

The purring cat repositioned himself more comfortably on Maggie's lap, and meowed in response to the sound of her voice.

'Prickly cactus? That's a bit harsh, Prowler, don't you think?'

★　★　★

'Aye, Calypso!' said Rocco as the redhead entered the gallery. Her hair was as bright orange as a clown wig and just as wild. Her tiny blue eyes scrunched up with a smile as she looked at him. She wore a patchwork prairie skirt in bright shades of purple, green, orange and turquoise with a tee top in a yellow bright as the sun. Huge earrings touched her shoulders and four necklaces hung long and tangled from her neck down to her heavy braless breasts. She was a walking color wheel that hurt the eyes. A hodgepodge of utter confusion. Not unlike the mysterious Misty, she too was a reflection of her art. Calypso was the collage artist who added vibrant, lively colors to the gallery walls and shelves. Her works were happy and made people smile. She collaged everything that came within her reach, from little boxes to clip boards to canvases to lamp bases. Nothing escaped her scissors and decoupage paste. Like a gypsy on the run, the proverbial packrat collected anything that shone or caught her eye. She lived at garage sales and thrift stores and scoured the alleyways on trash collection day. She ripped colors and patterns and faces from the pages of magazines with a manic fervor. Even the photographs on the newspapers obituary page weren't safe from her assault.

'Rocco, Rocco, Rocco!' She reached out for him, a myriad of bracelets clanked cacophonously as she embraced him. 'My roly-poly welcoming committee of one, give me a hug, you big cuddly-bear.'

With the attention span of a gnat Calypso looked around the room. 'Barbara, Adrian, Mary Rose!' Then she broke into a belly dance as she moved towards Armando and the bar. Shuffle, shuffle, kick, shimmy. 'Wine, let there be wine.'

'That's all she needs,' Adrian said to Rocco. 'Last month we nearly had to carry her out.'

'She's a free spirit.'

'She's as wacky as a jar of mixed nuts.'

Barbara Atwell walked into the second room to welcome customers. The gallery was filling fast, the conversation loud and rowdy, the body heat mixed with outside temperature, thick and stifling. She jacked up the air conditioner and stood before it, letting the chill breeze cool her before making another sweep of the room. It was an impressive turnout for this time of year and she was pleased.

Two familiar faces entered the room, eyes glazed and bloodshot as always. Crazy Jake held his beat up guitar with one hand and held onto Mouse's skinny arm with the other. Their flea-bitten cur followed obediently at their heels as they headed straight for the free food. Barbara would have banned them from the gallery a long time ago had it not been for the fact they always bought something. They were one step up from living on the street but they managed to buy Armando's little statues at every opening. She heard they lived in a rented garage somewhere in midtown and imagined their walls filled with those tacky little statues from Mexico. They were like focused hoarders who shared but one common fixation. And there was another plus. They would sit on the porch until closing time, Crazy Jake strumming his guitar and Mouse, jittery and pale from too many drugs, singing accompaniment. She had the voice of a siren that lured people off the street and into the gallery.

'Tonight I dance at the Oasis,' Calypso whispered to Armando, petting his arm suggestively. 'Why don't you meet up with me later?'

'Oh, *mi amiga*,' he replied. 'I have already made plans.'

'Arrogant jerk,' she said under her breath. 'You always have other plans.'

As Crazy Jake and Mouse neared the food table, Armando walked over to them, a good excuse to get away from the clinging Calypso.

'It is a pleasure to see you both,' he said. 'But the dog, she has to stay outside. It is no allowed you see.'

'Aw, 'mando,' Mouse said. 'Just this once, huh, huh?'

'Es no posseeb-lay,' he said. 'She is no my rules.'

With a shrug Jake took a square of cheese from the table and fed it to the dog. Then he handed it some crackers, which it downed hungrily. He took the leash from Mouse and headed to the front door, the dog drooling and coughing a path of crumbs in its wake.

'C'mon, Pooter,' Jake mumbled to the dog. 'It's under the tree time for you.'

A few people snickered as he passed.

'Shame on you, Jake,' said Mouse. 'You know her name is Pewter, like the color of her fur.' The dog was her baby and making fun of her name like that just wasn't nice. No matter how funny he thought it was. But her irritation

47

with him was as brief as her ability to focus.

'Hurry back,' she squeaked, her voice high and thin as she piled up all the food she could fit onto her plate. She wrapped more in a napkin and shoved it into her large purse. 'I'm waitin' right here for ya, Jake.'

Mary Rose walked slowly to the table and refilled her plate. 'You've such a lovely voice, my dear; will you be singing for us tonight?'

'Jake says I sing for my supper.'

'With that voice you deserve a feast.'

The flattery pleased Mouse. She was used to people looking at her as though she was contagious. Or averting their eyes completely as they walked by. Her clothes were dirty, she knew that, but given a choice between soap and feeding Pewter it was no contest. It was only when they played their music that people would stop and really notice them, a look akin to respect in their eyes. Like they were somebody. Like they had faces. They played for loose change that put a roof over their heads. And while it filled their pockets it also filled their hearts with joy. But mostly they played because it reminded them of who they used to be. Who they might have been if somewhere along the way they'd turned right instead of left.

'I like it here,' Mouse said as she shoved another bite of cheese into her mouth. 'People are nice to us here.'

Barbara sat at the desk giving change to a couple who'd just bought a music box. Calypso had likely found it at a garage sale, but when she was finished working her magic it was something new and wonderful. Re-purposing the tossed and forgotten and giving it a new life. Bringing pleasure to fresh eyes. And adding a little more to the till in the process.

'I will answer that,' said Armando as the phone rang.

Mary Rose couldn't help but overhear his end of the conversation.

'Oh, si, si,' he said. 'Is very busy and good. Why you are no here?'

He turned and faced away from the room as he continued, lowering his voice.

'How around midnight, my beautiful dove?'

Mary Rose's ears perked up.

'Is *no problema*. Until midnight then.' And he hung up.

'Paloma sends her apologies,' he called out to his wife. 'She is no feeling so well.'

Mary Rose returned to her chair in the corner of the room. She loved these receptions. It was like watching a free movie and she rarely missed a scene. There was a time she might have been the star player but those days were behind her and now she relished in the role of silent observer. It was damn near as much fun. But not quite mind you. Not quite.

She wondered why Armando felt he had to sneak around. It wasn't as though everyone didn't know. Most even participated. Barbara had plenty of her own action, truth be told, and made no secret of it. It was a given on both their parts. The Mosaic Gallery family was an open book with few, if any, secrets. Life was to be lived to the fullest, no holds barred, never stifled by other peoples rules. Their Bohemian enclave thrived with creativity and freedom, oblivious to the mundane world around them. They lived their own reality. And Mary Rose found this world far more appealing than the one that buzzed around mindlessly beyond its walls. Mary Rose had come to the conclusion that Armando was just sneaky by nature. She'd known his type over the years, even bedded a few. His secretiveness merely added to the mystique and fun of the game.

Crazy Jake re-entered the room, took Mouse by the elbow and steered her over to Armando's shelf. Armando joined them and Jake handed him a fistful of wadded up bills as Mouse reached for the statues. She put four of them into her purse as Armando counted the money and slipped it into his pocket. Three more people lined up by Armando and he quickly sold five more. What had been full shelves at the beginning of the night were now half empty.

Calypso floated into the room, her eyes flitting about with the attention span of a kid with ADD. She put the brakes on her erratic dance and jiggling breasts. Like a sputtering helicopter running out of gas she landed next to Mary Rose.

'This is getting boring,' said Calypso standing next to her. Once again she'd struck out with Armando. One of the few who had. 'Boring, boring, boring.'

Mary Rose looked up at her. 'You're perfectly right, my dear. I was just thinking as much myself. Could you give me a ride home perhaps?'

'I've got a gig later at The Oasis,' she said, doing a few hip thrusts to accentuate the point.

'Would that give you enough time to share a drink? And perhaps a little weed?'

'I wouldn't miss it,' she said as she helped Mary Rose to her feet.

The two women bade their farewells and walked arm in arm out the door and into the heat of the night.

★ ★ ★

Maggie Reardon kicked off the covers and the cat, then fell back to sleep. The night had been restless, mainly due to the heat but also because thoughts of

Marty were giving her monkey brain. They kept swimming around in her head and banging against her skull like balls careening around a pool table. As soon as she'd doze off another thought would jolt her awake again. She'd pegged him as a lot of things during their short affair, but his determination to win her back was both unexpected and a bit unnerving. She'd figured him weaker than that. But maybe it was that very weakness that was luring him back. Maybe he needed someone strong standing beside him to hold him upright. Maybe, maybe, maybe. Or maybe he wasn't who she thought he was at all. You think you know somebody but then you start to peel away the layers and discover you don't know them at all. But that's how it always is. People show you what they want you to see and keep the rest hidden under lock and key. Maybe she was no different. She hid things too. It was safer that way. Maggie was a good judge of people; you have to be when you're a cop. That's what keeps you alive. But this new wrinkle in Marty's character, or lack thereof, had her doubting herself. She could see right through people on the job, but when it came to her men she had a giant blind spot.

Plus she didn't like the fact that she was still physically attracted to him. Those blasted hormones!

Don't be silly, she reassured herself. You're jumping to conclusions and blowing this all out of proportion. Most of her ex-boyfriends ran in the other direction as fast as they could. And they never looked back. But this time a rejected lover shows up at the door with flowers, for God's sake! Most women would be flattered.

But Maggie wasn't most women.

She slept fitfully, waking up at the smallest of noises. More than once she thought she heard something outside the window, arose, and aimed the flashlight into the darkness. Nothing was there. But she felt edgy just the same. She told herself it could have been a passing coyote or javelina. Or pods falling from the green palo verde tree and onto the dry ground. It could have been anything. Or it could have been nothing at all.

So she wrote it off and went back to bed.

4

Bereavement in Blood

It was early morning in Tucson but the thick heat had already wrapped itself around Adrian Velikson and prickled her flesh like a rough wool blanket. She inhaled deeply and smelled the unwelcome scent of the wild fires that still burned uncontrollably to the south. She was up at five despite having left the gallery past eleven the previous night. Sometimes her sleep didn't last long. Like last night. She figured she might as well make good use of her time. Last night was more like a full-blown party than a reception and when things closed up both she and Barbara were too tired to clean up the mess. The tension between them seemed to have eased as the evening wore on and they'd even hugged each other at the end of the night, just like old times.

Maybe things would work out to her

liking after all. Or maybe she was just wishful thinking.

The sun peered cautiously over the horizon, already a flaming orange that presaged another day of unbearable heat. Adrian walked through the mosaic portal and up the porch steps. Ashtrays overflowed where they sat on the small tables. Empty and half-empty cups were scattered about and she saw her work was cut out for her before she ever got inside. She slid her spare key into the lock and pushed open the front door. Barbara would still be sleeping and Adrian wanted her to wake up to clean surroundings. It was the least she could do. It would please her friend. And more than anything she wanted to make Barbara happy, despite the strain on their relationship.

Perhaps because of it.

After cleaning she would catch up on the bookkeeping. Last night there had been more sales than expected and she looked forward to tallying up the figures. It was one more thing sure to bring a smile from Barbara.

In the first room she observed three empty spots on the wall where last night abstracts by Misty Waters had hung, silent and pale and lovely. Things were looking good. The gallery's interior was already too warm, so she proceeded to the second room and turned on the air conditioner. It gave one half-hearted clunk before it began to spit out cold air. If she was going to spend her morning working it was going to be in comfort, power bill be damned. There were plenty of areas where they'd had to cut back, but this wasn't going to be one of them. No sane person would live in the desert without air conditioning, and she wondered how the early pioneers managed to survive this hostile environment. Thick adobe walls had insulated them from some of the heat, but it wasn't until the advent of refrigerated air that people came in droves to settle here.

Adrian stood in front of the air conditioner and looked around the second room. There were a few more empty spaces on the walls, and four of the paintings wore sold stickers. Maybe The

Mosaic Gallery wasn't in such dire straits after all. She glanced through the doorway into the shadows of the third reception room. Something didn't look right. Even in the semi-darkness she could see that the shelves that held Armando's little statues were empty. She didn't remember his having sold them all when she'd left the night before. It puzzled her. She squinted and spotted something on the floor. Whatever it was, it was out of place. It looked like a pile of clothing, but what would Barbara's laundry be doing down here? And why on earth would she be washing clothes in the middle of the night?

Cautiously, Adrian walked into the room and flipped on the overhead lights. Below Armando's shelves lay a body. Cold and still and lifeless, arms outstretched like an invocation to the gods of mercy. It was the body of a man, the halo around his head a pool of coagulated blood, like some martyred saint in a crude religious icon. He was lying face down, head tilted to the side, but her eyes focused on the back of his bashed in head. Her body began to shake and her legs felt boneless and weak, unable to hold her. Adrian grabbed hold of the shelf to steady her balance and to digest the nightmare that lay at her feet. She realized she hadn't been breathing and inhaled a deep breath, which only made her feel more light-headed and dizzy. Even without looking at his face she knew who it was.

It was Armando.

Barbara's handsome Armando.

But as he lay there he was anything but handsome. Whoever had done this to him had seen to that. Armando had been a lot of things, a gigolo at best, an irritant at worst, but he certainly hadn't done anything to deserve this. As much as Adrian wanted the rogue to disappear she never would have wished for this.

Her instinct was to feel for a pulse, to look for some glimmer of life, but she didn't have to get any closer to see that he was gone. And by the looks of the rigor mortis he'd been dead for some time.

Dread overcame her as she realized she had to go upstairs and get his wife.

Barbara would be devastated, but at least she would be there to comfort her. She had always been there for her, through the best and worst of times, but this was *bad* beyond belief. Something like this just didn't happen. Not here. This place was a sanctuary. The Mosaic was a nurturing family that rose above the negativity that drove the outside world.

For the most part anyway.

But not any more, she thought as she looked down at the stiffening corpse. Somebody was capable of this, probably somebody she knew. But who? Her thoughts spun wildly. No, it had to be a stranger, an outsider. Maybe a robbery gone bad. That made a lot more sense of the senselessness of it all. Thoughts bolted through her head with the speed of monsoon lightning, leaping from one possibility to the next. Home invasions, she thought, were fueled by violence for violence sake and robbery was only the secondary motive. They happened all the time. That had to be it. That was senseless enough to make some sort of sense.

She'd have to look around and see

what was missing.

But first she'd have to wake up Barbara.

Oh my God, she thought. What if something happened to Barbara?

Adrian raced out the front door and around the back to the steps that led up to Barbara and Armando's private quarters. She took a deep breath, squared her shoulders and ascended the stairs, terrified of what she might find there.

* * *

The weight of Prowler on her chest, accompanied by his relentless howling, woke up Maggie Reardon from her latest nightmare. Sleep had been intermittent, but every time she dozed off she ended up in the middle of another bad dream. Her ex-husband was in one of them, ridiculing her, trying to make her feel inadequate. Every move she made was met with his disapproval, frustrating her and making her want to cry. But Maggie wouldn't cry. She refused to give him the satisfaction. Numerous ex boyfriends marched in and out of the other dreams, each one telling her off for one shortcoming or another. She wondered why it bothered her so much in her dreams while at the same time she didn't give any one of them a passing thought while she was awake.

Except for Marty.

In one of the dreams he was there, lurking in the shadows, watching her every move. Why, she kept repeating in the dream. Why?

'Nonsense!' she said, startling the cat as she jumped out of bed. 'Absolute nonsense.'

She threw on her robe and Prowler followed her into the kitchen, anxious for his first meal of the day. She opened a can of food for him, shook it into a bowl and set it on the floor. She almost tripped over him as she reached for the bag of coffee beans. Grinding her own was time-consuming but it was worth starting her day with the best. The coffee she got on the run had no more flavor than murky dishwater or warm piss, so her first cup of the day had to be a good one. While the brew percolated, she took the last stale donut from the box on the counter and shoved it into her mouth. Breakfast of champions. And lazy people. And cops.

She reached across the counter and turned on the radio.

' . . . expects to be another hot one, with temperatures threatening to break records . . . '

Maggie groaned, 'Great, just great.'

' . . . no rain on the horizon. Monsoon season's later than . . . '

She turned off the radio, disgusted. Pouring her first welcome cup of coffee, she hoped the day would be an uneventful one. Those nightmares had been enough action.

★ ★ ★

It was unlocked. Not a good sign.

Adrian Velikson's heart pounded as she opened the door and walked through the small sitting room in the upstairs apartment. When she reached Barbara's bedroom door it was closed. She stood there, afraid to open it for fear of what she might find on the other side. What if the killer, or killers, had come here first? What if Barbara lay dead beyond the closed door? What if she had lost her friend forever?

Tears burned her eyes as she reached for the door knob and slowly turned it. Cautiously, she opened the door and walked in. Barbara lay motionless in the bed, the hand-stitched quilt half covering her nude body. Adrian's worst nightmare had come true.

'Oh Barbara, no,' she said, closing her eyes.

Did she hear movement? Was she . . . ?

Adrian opened her eyes. One leg moved under the quilt as Barbara stretched her body into consciousness. She opened her eyes and blinked at the shadow that stood at the foot of her bed. She pushed the blonde hair away from her face and as her eyes focused she sat upright. She absent-mindedly pulled the quilt over her breasts and said, 'Adrian? Adrian, what are you doing here?'

'I . . . I . . . '

'What time is it?' Trying to collect her thoughts, Barbara looked at her friend and muttered, 'Adrian?'

'You need to dress.'

'What's going on?'

'Just get dressed, Barbara. You need to come downstairs.'

Barbara rose from the bed, reached across to the chair and slipped a caftan over her nude body. She instinctively walked over to the wall mirror to give her hair a quick brush.

'Put down the brush. This is no time for vanity, just hurry up.'

Adrian remained silent as Barbara followed her down the stairs and into the gallery. She found it impossible to verbalize the words. *Armando is dead.* She couldn't force herself to say it, as if not saying it made it not so. She took Barbara's hand as they entered the second room. Barbara pulled away from her grasp and ran into the third room, screaming.

'Armando! Oh my God, Armando,' she said, racing over and kneeling next to where his lifeless body lay on the floor. 'What happened? Adrian, what happened?' Tears streamed down her face as

66

she draped her body over his, ignoring the blood that stained her clothes and painted her strands of hair in the deepest shade of crimson.

Adrian walked over to her and lifted her to a standing position. She held her close and said, 'Stay away from him Barbara, there's nothing you can do.' Adrian gently pushed Barbara's hair from her face. 'It'll be okay, my darling. We'll get through this.'

'Okay? Nothing will ever be okay,' she said, stretching her arm toward her dead husband as Adrian firmly held her back.

'Don't. Touch. Anything. The police . . .'

'The police?'

'We have to call the police.'

'We have to call Rocco. Rocco will know what to do. Rocco always knows what to do.' She said the words as if she were chanting a mantra. 'Rocco will know, Rocco will know what to do.'

'Rocco will tell you to call the police.'

We have to . . . what happened?!'

'I found him like this. I don't know what happened. I just don't know.'

'You did it! You've always hated him.

You did it. You killed him.' She pulled away from Adrian and glared at her. 'You killed him, I know you did.'

The cruel words that spewed from Barbara's mouth stung worse than a scorpion. 'You know better than that. You're just upset. You know I could never hurt anything that you love. That would be like hurting you, and you know I could never hurt you.'

Barbara threw her arms around her friend and held her close. 'I'm sorry. I know better. I know you'd never hurt me. I'm so, so sorry. I just. I just . . . ' Staccato, unconnected words spilled from her mouth. They kept erratic time with her sobs as her shoulders shook in rhythm to her words and tearful gasps. She kept repeating, 'Armando. My beautiful Armando. My handsome Armando . . . '

* * *

The morning sun was already beginning to blister the blacktop as Maggie Reardon walked into the mini-mart to purchase her daily snack supply. She pushed through the glass door and greeted her friend.

'Ah, *mi amiga*,' Carlos said from where he stood behind the counter.

'*Buenos dias, Papacita*,' she replied.

'Is beautiful day, *sí*?'

'It's about as beautiful as standing inside a blast furnace. How can you stand it?'

'Too hot, too cold, it no matter much. We are alive and our stomachs are full. You were born here Miss Maggie, it should no bother you, *sí*?'

'I guess I must have a drop of Eskimo blood that my parents failed to tell me about. Every summer I swear I'm going to move away from here. Maybe go to the Pacific Northwest where it rains all the time.'

'Every year you tell me that. But you no go. I think you be sad away from your home.'

'Yeah, you're probably right,' she mumbled as she headed down the candy aisle. 'I'd miss you too much. But summer's here still stink big time!'

She knelt down by the rows of candy

bars and grabbed three, stood up and reached for some jerky. With her hands full she walked up front and spilled them onto the counter. Carlos looked at them with a smile and shook his head, making a tsk-tsk sound as he rang them up.

'You don't eat right, Miss Maggie,' he said.

'When my rear end starts to spread I might just have to think about that,' she said, giving her backside a slap. 'Until then, I've got other things to think about.'

'*Sí, sí,*' he said as he placed her items in a brown paper bag and handed them over to her.

'*Adios,*' she said with a wave of her hand as she pushed through the glass door and walked out to her squad car, squinting her eyes against the glaring sun.

Carlos whispered under his breath, 'My little Marguerita, she is *impossi-blay.*'

Maggie slid behind the wheel, turned on the ignition, reached over and pulled a random candy bar out of the bag. One was as good as the next. She unwrapped it and took a bite as she revved the motor and threw it into reverse. She had the fixes she needed to kick start her day. Caffeine. Nicotine. Chocolate. Maybe today would be calm and uneventful. She could use a little of that too. Just one day of cruising around the neighborhood with nothing to do beyond putting Otis Campbell in the drunk tank to sleep it off. Just one peaceful day in Mayberry with Andy and Opie and Aunt Bea. Hah, days like that only happened on television. But she could dream, couldn't she? Maggie shook it off. She fed on the adrenaline and excitement. Righting wrongs and catching the bad guys gave her life purpose, even if it was one never-ending battle after another. Come on, she thought, one day in Mayberry and I'd be bored to tears. Just like one day in the Pacific Northwest would probably have me complaining about the rain.

She shoved the last of the candy bar into her mouth and sucked the melting chocolate off her fingertips. She turned onto St. Mary's, heading in the direction of downtown Tucson. Men on bicycles peddled along the side of the road single file, in their skin tight pants and streamlined crash helmets; a homeless man pushed a shopping cart filled with soiled blankets and a clear plastic bag full of brightly colored feathers; under a bright purple awning, protected from the sun, people with blank expressions sat on a bench waiting for the next bus. Two college students in black concert tees walked slowly down the sidewalk, dragging their feet as they looked ahead with bloodshot eyes, hung over from last night's under-age reveling. There was nothing out of the ordinary, nothing to draw Maggie's attention.

It was proving to be a quiet morning in Tucson after all.

But it was still early.

Maggie continued driving east toward the tall buildings of downtown.

Static sputtered from the squad car radio and the voice at the other end was calling a possible Code 187. Maggie picked up and responded. She was only a few blocks from the address and was on her way.

5

Caliente de Muerte

The police tape wrapped around the outside perimeter of The Mosaic Gallery like a crazy yellow snake ready to constrict. The CSI van was parked in front as was Maggie's squad car. The place buzzed with activity as officers entered and exited the building. It was three hours since Maggie answered the call. Upon her arrival she had looked around at the empty cups and soiled paper napkins and dirty paper plates scattered around the rooms. Between sobs, Barbara Atwell had told her there was an opening night artist's reception the night before. She'd apologized for the mess, as though that should have been a concern as her dead husband's body lay lifeless in the next room. Maggie had escorted the two women who had called it in to the side yard and ordered them to stay put while she photographed the murder scene, looked around, and taped off the area.

While forensics dusted for prints inside the gallery, Maggie took her portable fingerprinting kit to collect prints from the women in the yard. Eventually, she would collect prints from everyone who'd touched the place, match them to the inside prints and see what was left once they were eliminated.

Back inside she looked at the trash left behind from the previous night. Eliminating that from the equation, the place looked clean. Too clean. Like someone had cleaned up *something*. But there had to be hundreds of fingerprints from dozens of hands. A lot of people had been in and out of these rooms, but the floor where the body lay almost looked as if it had been swept and scrubbed clean.

Except for the pool of blood surrounding the victim's head.

A 'south of the border' melody kept playing in Maggie's head with the cacophony of an out-of-tune mariachi band. *Caliente de Muerte*. A happy, uplifting melody with lyrics that defied the coldness of murder and loss. *Caliente de Muerte*, the warmth of death.

There was nothing warm about it.

Maggie had called in for forensics and the meat wagon on her way to the address.

Usually when faced with a scene like this, Maggie just went about her work, able to disassociate herself from the victim as she worked. But this time she kept turning back to look at him. Even in death, her first reaction was how handsome he was. How beautiful and animated he must have been in life. A shame really, but murder was always a shame wasn't it? Looking good doesn't make it any worse a crime or any more a tragedy. It always bothered her how on television, or in the papers, when the victim is pretty it always demanded more attention. As if being ordinary or plain made one unworthy of their time and coverage. *Beautiful co-ed disappears. Pretty little girl kidnapped. Handsome leading man dies of overdose.* Maggie knew it sold more papers, but it was unfair. Yet even as she thought those thoughts she looked over again at Armando's body. Those features, what she could see of them where he lay, could have belonged to a movie star.

The media was sure to love this one.

To Maggie, this crime was akin to destroying one of the works of art that hung on the gallery walls. He was marred, destroyed, ruined. Just like the side of a building defaced by some thoughtless graffiti thug determined to leave his mark. She hoped forensics would be able to find the mark left by his murderer. The small piece of evidence that would reveal his, or her, identity. In the meantime, she'd question everyone who'd touched this place to try and figure it out the old-fashioned way. And forensics would be the icing on the cake for a jury. It wasn't about making her world a better place. It never got better. It was about finding one iota of justice in all the madness. That was her job.

She sighed and got busy with the task at hand. She looked around the rooms unable to find anything that looked like a murder weapon. Anything heavy enough to have bashed in the vic's skull like that. A row of metal sculptures caught her eye. The figures were whimsical and made her smile. The little man heads were made of tin pie plates with washers or fat little bolts for eyes; soldered arms were made of kitchen knives and forks, while penises were formed from faucets and other phallic-shaped items she'd never quite seen that way before. Little statues of women stood among them also made of metal, breasts formed from dented tin cups, their pubic areas masses of twisted wire or rusted scouring pads. She didn't know squat about art, but she knew that she liked these. There was little joy to be found in her dark world but these made her smile. The sign on the wall above them bore the artist's name. Rocco La Crosse. La Crosse. Why did that name ring a bell? She couldn't quite place it, shook it off, and lifted a statue with her latex gloved hand and studied it. They were small, none of them heavy enough to do serious damage, much less bash in someone's skull. She laughed a little as she set it down and headed out the door.

The two women huddled together on a bench under a tree, right where she had left them. She'd question them later. As she was putting up the last of the crime scene tape a battered van pulled up and a stocky man jumped out and headed for the front gate. As he tried to enter, she informed him that he couldn't cross the line and stopped him.

'Please,' he said. 'Those are my friends. They called me to come and they need me to be with them.' He looked tough as nails with his tattoos and soiled jeans and scruffy beard, but his voice was soft and there was a gentleness in his eyes despite his obvious agitation.

'And you are?' Maggie asked, weakening.

'Rocco. Rocco La Crosse. They need me here. Please let me go to them,' he said.

So this was the creator of those amusing little naked people. Maggie couldn't help but smile at the thought of this rough-hewn fellow creating such delightful art. At first sight she'd have figured the closest he came to metal was working on somebody's junker for minimum wage. But nobody knew better than Maggie that first impressions can be deceiving. And she'd seen it all. A grieving father who ended up being the killer of his own child. A crack whore, mind turned to mush, who still knew right from wrong and turned state's evidence despite the danger. A society dame who slowly poisoned her husband with arsenic, then played an award worthy role as the devastated widow. And the volunteer coach, loved by all, who secretly photographed teenage girls as they undressed in the locker room.

First impressions can't be trusted.

People can't be trusted.

Not many of them anyway.

'Okay, but stay in the side yard,' she said, raising the tape to let him pass. 'Forensics is collecting evidence so don't go inside!' Then she added: 'I'll need to question you later. All three of you.'

Maggie watched the pony tail sway from side to side at the back of his head as he trotted toward the tree, one long earring banging against his neck as he approached the women. They rose and spoke to him.

'Somebody killed Armando,' Maggie heard the blonde say. Barbara Atwell, owner of the gallery, sobbed.

'Thank you for coming, Rocco,' said the short, stocky one who held Barbara's hand.

'I'm here now,' he said. 'Everything will be okay.' He reached out to them with muscled, hairy arms and embraced them both.

The three of them sat down on the bench under the shade of the palo verde tree.

Maggie didn't know where he fitted into the scenario, not yet, but she could see from the way they welcomed him that the man named Rocco was surely their 'rock.' Or could he be a co-conspirator? Or the lone killer? Her gut instinct told her otherwise, but for now everyone was a 'person of interest.' She would have to narrow it down until all that remained standing was the prime suspect. She didn't know where anyone fit in at this point. But sure as rattlesnakes had fangs she was going to find out.

★ ★ ★

'What are they doing?' Barbara Atwell asked as the forensics team marched up the stairs that led to her private apartment. 'That's where we live. Nothing happened up there.'

'They need to do their job,' Maggie Reardon said.

'Oh, I don't like this at all. It's like having somebody snoop in my diary,' she said. 'Barbara, Barbara,' Rocco La Crosse reassured her, 'they want to solve this, don't you?'

'Of course I do! It just makes me uncomfortable, that's all.'

'Then, like the nice detective says, let them do their job so they can get out of here.'

★ ★ ★

It was mid-afternoon by the time forensics wrapped up. They'd bagged up

81

any possible evidence, put it in the van and driven off. The body of Armando Salazar was also bagged and removed for autopsy. As they wheeled him out on the stretcher Barbara sobbed uncontrollably under the shade of the palo verde tree. The finality of it had hit her. Hard.

Maggie walked over to the tree, tired and wishing she were sitting at home in her comfortable chair with all of this behind her. Some days were longer than others and this was proving to be one of them. The sweltering heat didn't help.

'Let's go back inside,' she said to Barbara. 'I need to get a list of everyone who was here last night.'

'Everyone? I don't know everyone that was here.'

'Let's just do the best we can.'

Maggie and Barbara went inside, leaving Rocco La Crosse and Adrian Velikson behind. The gallery was still a crime scene and she didn't want to disturb it any more than necessary. Maggie had informed them that she wanted to speak to each of them, one at a time. But first she needed to get some sort of starting point as to who was present last night, when they left, and anything else that might be crucial to the investigation.

The cool breeze from the air conditioning hit the two women as they went inside and Maggie could feel the beads of perspiration on her face dry to salt. It felt good. They walked over to Barbara's desk and Maggie sat across from her, notepad in hand. Barbara removed a large address book from the top drawer and placed it on the desk in front of her. Her eyes wandered from Maggie to the floor of the next room then back again.

'Where do we start?'

'I'll need names, addresses, phone numbers,' Maggie said.

'I'll do my best but I don't know half of them. I guess I could start with the artists. At least I have information on them. I mean, other people come and go, some of them are regular customers, but for most of them I couldn't even furnish you with a name, much less an address.'

Even without her make-up and dressed in her shoddy, blood-stained caftan,

Barbara wore a regal and composed demeanor. Except for her occasional teary outbursts, which were certainly expected under the circumstances, she was handling things admirably.

'First I need to ask a few questions. When did you last see your husband?'

'Last night. When we were closing up. Armando kissed me goodnight because he was going out and I was exhausted. Then I went upstairs and went to bed.'

'Going out?'

'Armando is — was — high energy. He liked to party. If you haven't noticed, my husband was a bit younger. Being in his twenties he is — *was* — still in party mode. I hate to admit it, but at my age there's times I'd rather get a good night's sleep. Armando understood that.'

'That didn't bother you? I mean, him going out and leaving you behind?'

'Not at all. We're, we *were* married, but by no means did we *own* each other.'

'And you heard nothing after you went upstairs? A door closing? A commotion? The sound of a car engine perhaps?'

'Nothing. By the time my head hit the

pillow I was out cold. And I'm a heavy sleeper. When I was visiting friends in California I slept right through the Northridge earthquake.'

Then she added: 'I wish I'd heard something, anything. Maybe I could have . . . '

'Probably the only thing you'd have managed to do was to end up dead yourself. So don't even go there. Don't beat yourself up.'

'I don't know what to do. I don't know how I can help.'

'I understand you're under a lot of stress right now. Just do the best you can. You'll probably remember more details later. That's normal. If you do, just call me,' she said handing her a business card with her phone number.

The front door flew open, banging loudly against the wall. Both women jumped. A wild haired woman barged into the room with Rocco La Crosse close on her tail, yelling, 'You can't go in there!' He reached out and grabbed her by the arm as she neared Barbara.

'Belinda! I said you can't come in here.'

Turning to Maggie, he shrugged his shoulders and said, 'I'm sorry. I tried.'

'Wow, what happened?' said Belinda Blume, shoving the unkempt mop of hair from her eyes. 'I came to help clean up and there's friggin' yellow tape all over the place.'

'Armando's dead,' Rocco said to her. 'You really need to leave. I can fill you in outside.'

Belinda stretched her neck, looking into the third room, barely reacting to the pool of blood on the floor. 'Barb, I'm so sorry. Hey, you sold my Gaia! And look, all of Armando's stuff sold too.'

Ignoring Belinda's insensitivity, Barbara looked into the room. 'I didn't even notice before,' she said to the policewoman. 'It had to have been a robbery because those things didn't sell last night. They were stolen. But why would someone commit murder just for some statues? It really makes no sense.'

'*Just* some statues? Armando's maybe, but my Gaia is *art*,' said Belinda, 'who wouldn't want it? But Armando's?' She snorted. 'I'll get paid anyway, won't I?

Even if it was stolen instead of sold?'

Barbara was losing patience, her throat tightening so that she could barely speak. 'I'm insured. You'll get paid at the end of the show like you always do.'

'Well, that's a relief.'

Maggie was trying to read the fleeting expression in Belinda Blume's eye. Was it amusement? Disdain? This broad was some piece of work and she could hardly wait to sit her down and grill her. 'Do I have to escort you out myself or are you going to leave?' she said.

'C'mon,' said Rocco giving her a firm shove in the direction of the door.

As they left the room, Maggie heard him say, 'My god, Belinda. Sometimes I can't believe what comes out of that nasty mouth of yours. Barbara's husband is dead and all you care about is your damn Gaia?'

'I put a lot of work into that piece. Besides, it was *only* Armando.'

'Belinda!'

At the sound of the door slamming Barbara returned her attention to the detective that sat across from her, fresh tears welling in her eyes. 'I guess we don't need that list now. If it was a robbery . . . '

'Robbery is only one possible scenario, albeit an interesting one. My job is to investigate every possible avenue. Hopefully we'll have a few answers once the forensic reports come in.' Then gently she added, 'And the autopsy results.'

Well, that sure triggered the old waterworks, Maggie thought as Barbara wiped her hand across her wet cheek. 'This is going to be very embarrassing for the gallery. Can you imagine what my customers will think when they're questioned? About a murder?' Her hands shook as she angrily flipped to another page in her address book. 'I couldn't think of more devastating PR if I'd purposely planned to destroy The Mosaic Gallery all by myself.'

* * *

Maggie Reardon walked out the gallery door, notebook in hand. It had been like pulling teeth but she had a good list of names to follow up on. Barbara Atwell was two paces ahead of her, heading to the tree where Rocco and Adrian Velikson sat. They rose and wrapped their arms around their friend in a group hug.

'They won't even let me stay here,' she said. 'The entire gallery is considered a crime scene.'

'You can stay with me,' said Adrian. 'I can squeeze you in.'

'I think it's better she stay with me,' said Rocco. 'I have plenty of extra room.'

'You're right. You're always right,' said Adrian, thinking of the cramped little studio apartment she'd moved into around the time Armando and Barbara had married. There was barely enough room in the 500-square-foot bachelor pad for one, let alone two. What she'd thought of as a temporary move had become more permanent as the weeks turned into months of waiting. For the call that never came.

Barbara turned to Maggie Reardon. 'My purse, clothes, everything is upstairs. Can't I at least take some things with me?'

Maggie accompanied her up the back stairs and into the apartment, watching her every move as she packed her make-up and shoved as many clothes as would fit into her overnight bag. Before they headed back down, she had Barbara slip out of the blood-soaked caftan. Even Maggie was awed by the statuesque beauty of this woman. It was no wonder a younger man had found her irresistible. She reminded Maggie of a pale ice princess from one of the old Alfred Hitchcock thrillers. Cool and collected. Doing her best to maintain her composure under the worst possible circumstances. Maggie picked up the caftan and slipped it into a large evidence bag. Forensics would check it out, see if there was tell-tale blood spatter or if the blood had soaked into it as Barbara Atwell knelt down and held her dead husband, as both she and Adrian had stated.

Maggie locked the door and pocketed the keys as she and Barbara descended the stairs to her waiting friends. At least she has a good support system, Maggie thought. She's going to need it.

The day was nearly over. Dark shadows spread their elongated fingers across the side yard and touched the front gate. The air remained thick with the day's heat and wouldn't let up even as the sun set, the darkness only providing the illusion of coolness. Instead of sunny and sweltering it would be dark and hot. It was on days like this Maggie wished she had a swimming pool instead of a cold shower. Or that she could sit under the towering pines by a lake somewhere, far from the desert, inhaling the welcome scent of falling rain.

When she approached them with her portable fingerprint kit to ask for their prints they cooperated. She gave them each her card with her precinct and cell phone numbers and told them to call if they thought of anything. Then Maggie Reardon lifted the yellow crime scene tape and the three of them ducked under leaving the gallery, and the crime scene, behind them. Rocco La Crosse took the overnight bag from Barbara and slung it over his broad shoulder as the three of them headed towards his van. He turned and looked at her and as their eyes met something in Maggie's stomach fluttered.

I don't get it, she thought to herself. He isn't even my type. But those little butterflies hinted otherwise. She returned his smile then headed for her squad car, cursing herself. Cursing her body for reacting the way it did.

This man, after all, was a possible suspect.

6

One Step Forward, Two Steps Back

The aroma from the bucket of fried chicken filled Maggie's car, reminding her she hadn't eaten since morning. She'd picked it up at a drive-thru and sat it on the passenger's seat with a side of slaw, some potato salad, and a buttered biscuit. Her stomach growled. Maybe a real meal would ease the hunger pains that gnawed away at her gut, keeping uneasy company with the mystery of her unsolved murder. One out of two. She would fill her stomach tonight and let the murder at The Mosaic Gallery take a back seat until tomorrow.

The glare of the setting sun reflected its blinding light across her dusty windshield as she headed west toward home. She reached over and turned on her wind-shield wipers, squirting water across the glass as the blades did their best to scrape away the dirty film. Beads of water splashed into the open driver's side window and slapped against the side of her face. She ran her hand across her wet cheek, turned off the wipers, rolled up the window and jacked up the air conditioning.

The melody and lyrics of *Caliente de Muerte* played over and over in her head. The warmth of death fought its battle against the Tucson heat and the hum of the air conditioner.

Maggie pulled into her driveway, turned off the ignition, grabbed the bag full of chicken and headed for the front door. As she shoved her house key into the lock, she noticed a note tacked onto the door with a purple push pin.

Written across the bright yellow envelope, perfectly centered in a familiar script, was her name. She'd know Marty's handwriting anywhere. Small, precise and scratchy. Damn near obsessive/compulsive in its neatness, as straight as if it had been written on perfectly lined paper. She pushed her way through the door and walked to the kitchen, Prowler fast on her heels, meowing in unison to the beat of her footfalls.

'You could at least welcome me home,' she said. 'It would be nice to know I'm wanted for more than just filling your gut.' She reached into the bag and removed a chicken breast. She pulled off a chunk, tore it into bite-sized pieces and threw it into Prowler's dish. He started attacking it before the dish hit the floor.

'Where are your manners? Were you born in a barn?' Then she smiled to herself. Prowler had indeed been born in a barn. She'd picked him out of an abandoned litter at a crime scene, the only kitten who still had a spark of life in him. She had patiently hand fed him with an eye dropper, slowly nursing him back to health. You'd think he would show some gratitude, she thought, but what can one expect from a cat? 'Your lack of breeding is showing,' she said as he gulped down the last of the chicken.

Maggie walked back across the living room to the front door, opened it, and pulled the envelope from where it was pinned. On the corner of the envelope was a floral sticker. What's with Marty and his damn little pink flowers? Slamming the door behind her, she sat the envelope on the side table and returned to the kitchen. Prowler was on the counter, half way inside the bag of chicken. She pulled him out and he growled in protest as she wrestled away the thigh that he held tightly between his sharp teeth.

'This is *my* dinner, you little brat,' she laughed, throwing the piece of chicken back into the bag. 'First things first,' she said to herself as she opened a can of cat food for him. He looked at the sloppy tuna in his dish and up to the counter, disappointment registering in his stubborn green eyes.

Maggie placed her food in the oven, out of his reach, then changed into the comfort of her ratty bathrobe before returning to the kitchen. She dished out a heaping plateful, flipped on the television, and settled into her chair.

'Bad boys, bad boys,' droned the television with the theme song of *Cops*.

'Whatcha gonna do when they come for you?'

'You're gonna cower and cry for your mother,' Maggie said to the set.

She worked her way through the coleslaw, potato salad, and chicken, tossing pieces onto the floor to appease Prowler while she ate. She'd forgotten how good a full stomach felt, but there was still a corner of her gut that churned restlessly as she thought of the handsome corpse that lay on the gallery floor. And something else was stirring too. Something she preferred not to acknowledge. She pushed it from her mind, returned to the kitchen and emptied the bones into the trash can under the sink, out of her cat's reach.

Maggie poured herself an Irish, threw in a few ice cubes, and settled back into her chair. She reached over to the side table, pulled a cigarette from the pack, lit it, inhaled, and sighed. She put her feet up on the ottoman and settled back. The yellow envelope sat by the pack of cigarettes silently demanding her attention. Might as well get it over with she thought, reaching over and lifting it from the table. She tore it open. It was one of those mushy greeting cards with a muted photo on the front of a couple walking along the beach at sunset. All in shades of gray and ochre and browns. Give me a break, she thought. As if it couldn't get worse, inside was a silly verse about love and missing you and somehow the hack poet had managed to make the thoughts rhyme. Love and above. Romance and dance. Miss you and kiss you. It was almost as pathetic and irritating as that little bouquet of flowers he'd left at her doorstep.

How in the world had she ever hooked up with him? But she remembered exactly how. How easy it had been for two mismatched souls to think they were right for each other in the midst of passion. It had worked just fine. For a while. The memories of their lovemaking made her uncomfortable, not because it wasn't good, but because it was. It had been close to magical. But everything else in their relationship was off-kilter. Oil and water. Square pegs and round holes all the way.

But even so, she found herself yearning for the comfort of a body next to hers.

The sound of the telephone ringing snapped her back from her reverie.

'What?' she said into the receiver.

It was Marty, his voice soft and seductive.

Maggie felt the same fluttering below her waist that had been bothering her intermittently ever since she had left the gallery. It had been fairly easy to push it aside until now. The sound of Marty's voice brought it all to the surface despite her efforts to ignore it. She cursed those sneaky hormones, knowing they'd get the best of her. They were nothing but nature's little dirty trick to keep the world populated. Well, a good supply of birth control pills had outsmarted nature on that one!

'I've missed you so much,' he was saying. 'If we could just talk, maybe we could work this out.'

She didn't say much as she listened. She was too busy trying to fight the temptation with his blond hair and irresistible blue eyes and perfectly toned body. And memories of him lying next to her.

'Maggie, are you still there?'

'I'm still here, Marty.'

Pause.

'Marty? Come on over and we'll talk it over.'

'I'll be right there.'

'Give me an hour, okay?'

'If I have to,' he said, his voice reflecting his unwarranted optimism.

'And Marty . . . '

'Yes?'

'It's only to talk. You got it?'

But they both knew better.

★ ★ ★

Maggie cleaned the cat's box in the bathroom, poured in fresh litter and kicked it below the pedestal sink. She carried the bag of stinky, urine soaked sand outside to the trash bin and tossed it in. The sun had lowered itself beyond the far side of the mountains. Bats were flitting erratically in the semi-darkness above her head in their nightly search for insects.

Despite not being frightened by them, she couldn't help but duck with their every passing swoop. It was instinct. Nothing more. She ran back into the house and took a quick shower, then slipped into something that didn't say 'I have to have you' but would be easy enough to slip off if her hormones out-witted her common sense. If instinct overcame reason. She still hadn't come to terms with her true motive in inviting Marty over. Why she was caving in after she'd made it clear to him, as well herself, that their relationship was over. It was only to talk, she told herself as she sprayed his favorite perfume between her breasts.

★ ★ ★

Maggie and Marty hadn't talked very long before they were headed to the bedroom.

And now, passion spent, Maggie was already having regrets. Why, while they had been in the throes of passion, was she fantasizing about another man? A man with a scruffy beard and arms covered in tattoos. In the looks department there was no comparison, but Rocco La Crosse kept wedging himself into her thoughts nonetheless.

She lay in bed staring at the ceiling while her perspiration soaked into the sheets beneath her. She didn't like where this was going. Not one bit. She didn't like having Marty back in her bed nor did she like having thoughts about someone she could never get involved with. At least she still had that much sense about her.

Marty was settled in next to her, lying on his side, already half asleep. She nudged him.

'Huh?'

'You have to go now.'

'But I thought we . . . '

'It's getting late and I'm tired.' Already he was starting to suck up all her oxygen and she was finding it difficult to breathe. Why did he always make her feel like that? Like he'd chained her inside a tiny cage and wouldn't let her escape. As if he'd never be content unless he totally possessed her.

'Marty,' she began, then stopped mid-sentence. She never should have asked him over. She was stirring up the same mess that she'd put behind her. And for what? A few moments of pleasure and release? She'd have been way ahead of the game if she'd just settled for an alternate, and far safer, method. No strings attached.

'You really need to go now.'

Reluctantly, he got out of bed, dressed and left.

★　★　★

About three in the morning, Maggie awoke with a start to a rustling sound coming from the kitchen. Cautiously, she slid out of bed and reached for the revolver on the nightstand. She slipped silently into her robe in the darkened room and tiptoed towards the kitchen. As she entered the room she flipped on the light and cocked her gun, aiming it in the direction of the sounds.

'Darn you,' she said, uncocking the gun and setting it on the kitchen table. Prowler looked at her from where he sat by the open cabinet door beneath the sink. He was scrunching chicken bones with a look of smug defiance. 'Don't you know those things can kill you?'

Maggie stooped down and shoved the scattered bones back into the trash bag as Prowler fought her for one more piece. And failed. She should have taken them out when she went out earlier.

But her mind had definitely been elsewhere.

She pulled a tiny piece of remaining meat off a leg bone and tossed it across the floor. Prowler attacked it as if it were a mouse and gobbled it down with a growl. Maggie slipped out the back door, trash bag in hand and threw it into the trash bin. Slamming down the lid she looked up and was awed at the sight. A million stars splashed across the night sky like scattered diamonds shimmering against a black velvet backdrop. It was beautiful, she had to admit.

But her practicality won out. She'd

have preferred seeing clouds. No such luck. There wasn't a hint of monsoon rains in the sky. And that meant another hot day with no relief in sight.

She turned to head back into the house when a sound from the alleyway caught her attention. It sounded like it was coming from just beyond her back fence. Like footsteps. But who would be out walking in the middle of the night? Unless they were up to no good. She wished she'd brought her flashlight out with her. As well as her gun. She walked across the rocky yard toward the fence, dodging the random cactus that lurked along the pathway. When she got to the fence she stopped and listened, holding her breath.

All was silent.

Slowly, she raised herself on her tiptoes and peered over the wall.

There was nothing there.

Nothing but the darkness below and the stars overhead.

Maggie Reardon kicked herself for being so jumpy and headed back to the house. It was probably nothing but some horny old stray looking for a little action.

There seemed to be a lot of that going around tonight. Maybe it had something to do with the position of the stars or the stifling heat. Well, whatever the cause it was contagious and running rampant. She smiled, hoping the old guy would find what he was looking for.

She still had time for a few more hours sleep.

7

Cannabis and Chamomile Tea

Detective Maggie Reardon pulled up to the curb in front of a typical Arizona ranch house. The stucco was painted ochre with trim a combination of deep purple and mint green. Several rose bushes lined the front walkway and a Texas Ranger plant sprawled under the picture window, pregnant with hundreds of tiny lavender flowers.

The place looked cozy and inviting.

Maggie flipped through her notes before exiting the car, briefcase and portable fingerprint kit in hand. She had called Mary Rose earlier that morning to set up a time for a visit. The voice on the other end of the phone had been animated and pleasant. Maggie liked questioning people in their own surroundings. Not only did it make them more comfortable and relaxed, but more often than not seeing how a person lived told her a lot more about them than anything that came out of their mouths in an interrogation room.

She walked up to the front door and rang the bell.

The door opened a crack and an elderly woman peered out at her with a twinkle in her eyes.

'You must be Detective Reardon,' she said as she opened the door. 'Do come in, dear, you must be sweltering out there.'

The room was neat as a pin, but as soon as Maggie entered she detected the faint smell of stale marijuana smoke and cat urine. Not overwhelming, but definitely there, lurking just under the surface. The soft aroma of Blue Waltz perfume floated in the air ever so faintly. The sense of smell, the most powerful memory trigger, flashed images of her mother tucking her in at bedtime. And the room was filled with the scent of freshly baked cookies. Childhood memories wrapped around her like a cozy blanket.

She immediately felt comfortable here.

'Do sit down,' said Mary Rose, indicating a chair with white crocheted doilies on the arms and back. The room reminded Maggie of an English country cottage right out of a BBC mystery. Watercolors filled the sage green walls, mostly flowers and rural scenes in muted shades of lilacs and greens. Each bore the signature of Mary Rose. She shook hands with the elderly woman, properly introduced herself, then settled down into the chair.

'Where are my manners?' asked Mary Rose. 'I just put on a nice pot of chamomile tea. May I offer you a cup?'

'That would be nice, thank you.' This darling woman had a comfortable, relaxed aura about her.

As Mary Rose headed to the kitchen Maggie asked if she could assist.

'No, no, no my dear, everything's under control.'

A white Persian cat trotted across the room and jumped onto Maggie's lap to check her out. It sniffed her face and tickled her ears with its whiskers and started to purr, then settled onto her lap like they were old friends, dropping little tufts of fur on her navy blue pants.

'You're definitely sweeter than the ungrateful fellow I have at home.'

'Ah, so you've met Sir Chesterfield,' Mary Rose said as she returned to the room and set the tea tray on the coffee table. 'I can see you've passed muster.'

She handed Maggie a small plate with three home baked cookies and a linen napkin, then poured the hot brew into teacups. 'Cream and sugar?'

'Two sugars.'

Mary Rose placed the cup of tea on the side table next to Maggie, then sat down on the love seat across from her and took a long, slow sip from her own dainty cup.

'I was shocked when you called this morning and told me the purpose of our little visit. It's so hard to imagine Armando not with us. Why, I just saw him last night and he was so, well, alive.'

'Did you know him well? Anyone who might have wanted to hurt him?'

'I tend to keep my mouth shut and my ears open. One gets all kinds of little tidbits that way, but no, I can't imagine anyone wanting to actually hurt him.'

'Actually?'

'Oh, he liked to play the charmer. And he played people. He liked to play a lot of things. He was quite the player, Mr. Armando. And a first-class lothario, but,' she ran knobby, arthritic fingers through her white hair and thought for a minute before continuing. 'I doubt anyone took offense. My goodness, he's bedded half the gallery, but nobody took him seriously. This probably isn't nice to say, but he was, well, sort of a community plaything at Mosaic.' She chuckled.

'Did his wife know? About the affairs I mean.'

'Barbara? She was blind in love where Armando was concerned, but sure she knew. And he knew about her as well. It was no big deal. They may have been married, but they had an understanding. It was a very open relationship.'

'So Barbara had lovers too?'

'At least two that I know of. No, probably just one. Rocco La Crosse stopped seeing her *that way* once she was married.'

'Why was that?'

'It wouldn't have mattered to Barbara, but Rocco has his own rules, and not messing with married women is one of them. You know, Rocco's the best friend a person could have. And they're still the best of friends. Benefits or no.'

'And the other lover?'

'Oh, that would be Adrian,' she said.

Maggie flipped through her notes.

'Adrian Velikson?'

'You look surprised.'

Maggie cleared her throat. Barbara Atwell was so feminine that the idea had never crossed her mind.

'Do you think Adrian was jealous?'

'Of course she was jealous. How would you feel if someone you'd been lovers with since college turned around and got married? It took her awhile, but she's accepted it.'

'Maybe not so much . . . '

'Oh, Detective Reardon, if you're thinking Adrian is capable of murder, you're mistaken. Adrian is one of the gentlest souls I've ever met.'

Maggie tried to wrap her head around that one. Gentle wouldn't have been the first adjective that came to mind to describe the butch little broad she'd met yesterday at the gallery.

Mary Rose chuckled, sipped her tea and nibbled on her cookie, then set the cup down on the saucer. 'Let me tell you about Adrian,' she said. 'Adrian is like a roasted marshmallow. She's crusty as a burnt biscuit on the outside but all soft and mushy on the inside.'

Maggie would let that go for now. After all, Adrian Velikson had the oldest motive in the world. Jealousy.

'Did you notice anything out of the ordinary last night? Anyone not familiar?'

'There's always a few new faces, but no, nothing that stood out really.' She thought for a minute. 'Oh, I do remember one thing.'

'Yes?'

'Armando was on the telephone with Paloma Blanca. They made plans to meet up after the show. But obviously he didn't make it if you found the poor man dead at the gallery.'

'Paloma Blanca? That name isn't on my list.'

'She wasn't there last night. Oh, she makes lovely jewelry. She can do things with silver and semi-precious stones that are magical. Paloma made this ring,' she said, holding out her hand to display her dramatic carnelian ring.

'It's beautiful,' said Maggie, looking at the ring Mary Rose held out so proudly. 'Would you happen to have an address or phone number for her?'

'I've got it around here somewhere.' She started to rise.

'That's okay, I'll get it from you before I leave. And I'll need to get your fingerprints, too.'

'Oh my. Does that mean I'm a suspect?'

'It's only for purposes of elimination.'

'If you think it might help.'

'Do you remember what time you left the gallery last night?'

'It was early. I tire faster than I used to. I think it was around eight-thirty. Calypso was all pissed off because Armando snubbed her advances again and she asked me for a ride home.'

'The two of you left together?'

'Yes, we came back here for a little wine and conversation.'

'And a little pot?'

Mary Rose's laughter was like the sound of tinkling bells. 'Oh, you are a good detective. I might be old but believe me I'm not dead yet. Just because there's snow on the roof . . . why I could tell you about my years in Paris that would make the antics at The Mosaic Gallery look like amateur hour.' Her attention drifted as her mind wandered off to the Left Bank of Paris. Then she snapped back to the present. 'But I'm sure you're not here to bust me over a little medicinal pot, are you dearie?'

'Negative.'

Maggie stroked Sir Chesterfield's white fur as he slept on her lap. She was liking Mary Rose more by the minute. Mary was straight forward and up front, which was refreshing compared to most of the people she dealt with. She drained the last of her tea from the cup and sat it down on the side table.

'Your perfume, that's Blue Waltz, isn't it?'

'Why Detective Reardon, you're way too young to remember Blue Waltz. When I was in grade school I'd save my allowance and buy it at the five-and-dime. By the time I could afford the expensive stuff I was too hooked on it to trade up. It's no longer easy to find, but it's still out there on the internet. How, pray tell, are you familiar with such an old-fashioned scent?'

'It's the perfume my mother wore.'

'I can see in your eyes that you loved her very much. Would it be improper to ask how you lost her so young?'

'My parents were driving back from Phoenix when a haboob kicked up. The sandstorm was blinding, maybe five percent visibility. They were rear-ended by a semi truck. I lost them both that day.'

'How tragic.'

'It was, yes. I was just two months into eighteen, so at least I didn't end up in the system.' Maggie had stayed in their house, managed the payments by working in a fast food joint, and kept the land-line listed under their names. As irrational as

116

it seemed, she saw it as a way of keeping them close. She changed the subject. 'I might need to speak with you again.'

'To pick my brains?' asked Mary Rose with a twinkle.

'That, too,' she said. 'But I also enjoy your company.'

'That would be lovely.'

★ ★ ★

Maggie sat in her car, checking her notes, and looking across the street to Viente de Agosto Park. The thermometer was hovering just below 105 degrees and threatening to go higher, so she kept the engine running for the air conditioning as she flipped through her pages. Barbara Atwell had told her she would find two of the regular gallery patrons here. She had no address for them. And she didn't have much in the line of names for them either. Just Crazy Jake and Mouse.

She jotted down a few more questions she needed to ask the gallery owner then closed her tablet.

Maggie turned off the ignition, exited

the car and walked across the street. A scruffy-looking man with a beard that looked like it was breeding cockroaches was sitting with a petite woman nearly as disheveled as himself. They sat with a large, lazy dog under the tall statue of Pancho Villa. The man strummed his guitar, the open guitar case on the ground in front of him, silently begging donations. Barbara had furnished a good description. He was definitely Crazy Jake. The two of them looked homeless and lost. As Maggie neared them, she could hear the music. The woman Barbara Atwell had called Mouse was singing an old Joan Baez folk song in a clear and beautiful voice. The occasional passerby would toss a few coins or a bill into the guitar case, never slowing their pace as they walked by. They didn't stop but they should have. With a gift like that Mouse should have been charging admission.

Maggie reached into her pocket and pulled a five dollar bill from her wallet. They smiled at her as she dropped it into the guitar case. She waited until the song ended before she spoke. As she introduced herself Mouse's mouth twitched nervously and Jake looked at her with suspicion.

'Are you here to bust us?' asked Mouse in a squeaky voice, nervously twisting her matted hair.

Maggie wondered how she could sing so beautifully yet have a speaking voice as annoying as fingernails on a chalk board.

'You must be Jake,' she said to the guitar player. He ignored her. She sat on the ground next to them and crossed her legs, trying to look non-threatening to this pair that obviously had issues with authority.

'Barbara from the gallery told me I could find you here. I just wanted to ask you a few questions about the other night.'

'The reception? We never miss the reception. But we didn't do nothin' bad,' said Mouse nervously. 'It's okay if I took some food. It's free, just ask Miss Barbara. She always lets me take some extra cuz I sing for her.'

'You sing beautifully, too,' said Maggie.

'Jake, she thinks I sing pretty. Ain't that nice Jake, huh?' She smiled like a Cheshire cat, exposing a row of discolored teeth as Jake continued to eye her with suspicion. 'It's okay, Jake, she's a nice lady, I can tell. She says I sing good.'

'Sometimes you're simple,' he said.

'That ain't very nice, Jake.'

The dog rose and stretched, then ambled lazily over to the side of the statue. He lifted his leg and pissed on Pancho Villa, reflecting the sentiments of half the citizens of Tucson to this odd gift from Mexico. Like so many other things in this town, *Señor* Villa was a point of contention, some people hating it, others finding a statue honoring a Mexican outlaw an appropriate addition to the landscape. Maggie thought it made about as much sense as if Chicago were to erect a statue in honor of A1 Capone. But she was a cop and had a definite bias against the bad guys. The dog lowered his leg, trotted back and plopped down next to Jake.

'Something terrible happened at the gallery night before last and I just need to ask you a few questions.'

'What are you talking about?' asked Jake, finally acknowledging her.

'Armando Salazar was murdered. His body was found in the gallery yesterday morning. Did you know Armando?'

Mouse began to cry and her crying turned into high pitched shrieks.

''Mando is our friend,' she cried. 'Oh 'Mando. Jake, what are we going to do without Armando?' Her demeanor edged on frantic as she clutched Jake's arm and buried her face in his shoulder. 'What are we gonna do without our 'Mando?'

'Shhh,' he said. 'Just shut up, will you?'

'But Jake . . . '

'Who would want to kill Armando?' he asked Maggie. 'Have you caught him yet?'

'We're working on it.'

Mouse was still weeping, the dog looking at her with confused, sad eyes.

'Do you remember what time you left the gallery, Jake?'

'I don't wear a watch, lady. I don't care much what time it is. Time is nothing more than a trap to make the masses march in time for the man. It's a concept with no meaning.'

'I know,' said Mouse, her face lighting up at the thought of being useful. 'We play our music on the porch and we stay until it closes.'

'And what time was that?'

'I dunno, when it closes, that's all.'

Maggie checked her notes. 'Ten.'

'Yea, ten, that's it.'

Sitting on one of the rare patches of grass in Tucson, Maggie's eyes were starting to water and her skin was starting to itch. She was allergic to every kind of grass that grew and the lack of grass in Tucson was a blessing. She knew she'd never survive up in Phoenix where they plant lawns everywhere, the over-usage of water be damned. Phoenix looked down on Tucson more than just geographically. They found Tucson backward and uncivilized. Maggie found it practical and down to earth. Water was a precious commodity, not to be wasted on lawns. Tucson was unique. Phoenix was trying to look like any big city anywhere and was succeeding. It lacked Tucson's character. She scratched her arm, then released a sneeze like a burly truck driver, causing Jake to jump.

'Bless you,' said Mouse.

'What's the matter with you, Mouse? What'dya want to be blessing a cop for?'

'Cuz it's polite, Jake, and if you haven't noticed I'm a lady!' She sat up straight and squared her shoulders proudly, trying to maintain a semblance of dignity in her worn rags. 'I'm a lady and don't you forget it.'

Jake patted the dog on the head, ignoring her.

'I'm sorry Jake,' she whined. 'I didn't mean nothin'.'

'Sometimes you just talk too much.'

'But Jake,' she said. 'You never told me what we're gonna do without Armando.'

'You'll be fine,' he whispered. 'Ain't I always taken good care of you? Just shush up. People die all the time. Armando ain't no different.'

'But he was our friend.'

The grass was starting to raise hives around Maggie's ankles and the conversation was going nowhere fast.

Maggie determined this wasn't the

time to ask for prints. Not with Jake's paranoia filling the air. 'Tell you what,' she said. 'I'd really like to talk to both of you some more. Do you have an address where I could see you another time?'

'What, do we look like we don't have an address? We ain't street bums.' Jake was on the defensive and itching for some sort of altercation to prove his suspicions about 'the man.' The perceived enemy.

And Maggie wasn't about to take the bait.

'No, I never thought that for a minute. I just thought we might all be more comfortable were we to meet more privately.'

'So you can bring in the Gestapo to tear our place apart? I don't think so,' said Jake.

Mouse lowered her eyes and pouted.

'Just me. I promise,' said Maggie.

'She's okay, Jake,' Mouse whined in his ear.

Maggie could see the paranoia dancing in Jake's eyes. She'd seen it a hundred times in as many faces. Looking at him, she fully understood why everyone referred to him as Crazy Jake. She'd had to hold back a few times from calling him that herself. And Mouse? The woman thought Jake was her protector, but it was obvious to Maggie that things were really the other way around.

Maggie handed Mouse her card.

'And do you have a number where I can reach you?' Maggie asked.

'I don't believe in telephones,' Jake said. 'They put little things in them so they can listen in and spy on you.'

'And they record everything you say,' said Mouse. 'Jake told me so.'

'Then I'd say it's perfectly understandable that you don't have one,' Maggie said to Jake, then added, 'One can't be too careful.'

This conversation was going downhill faster than a junk bond.

'I'd appreciate if both of you would think about the reception the other night, see if you remember anything that might help us catch the person who murdered Armando Salazar. My number's on the card.'

'Wow,' said Mouse. 'You mean I'd be

like a deputy or something?'

'Absolutely.'

Mouse shoved the business card into her purse and looked at Maggie, eyes wide. 'If I helped find 'Mando's killer I'd be really special, huh?'

'The way you sing I'd say you're already pretty special.'

Mouse beamed.

'Could I have your address?' Maggie asked her.

'No,' said Jake. 'Unless you want to arrest us for something, where we live ain't none of your business. I know my rights and you can't mess with them.'

'I don't know if it has a number,' said Mouse.

'Shut up,' said Jake, exasperated.

Ignoring him, Mouse continued. 'If you go down Convent Street, we live over there. It's the only bright yellow garage door on the whole street. It's as bright as sunshine or maybe somebody's pet canary. It's only a garage, but I like it there. I made it pretty, didn't I Jake?'

'Damn it Mouse. Why didn't you just draw the pig a friggin' map?'

126

'Don't be so rude, Jake. She's being really nice to us.'

'Pigs just pretend they're nice when they want something. Didn't I teach you nothin' at all?'

Crazy Jake was like a throwback to the hippie days. Did people even call cops pigs anymore? She'd been called a lot of things but couldn't remember ever having been called a pig. Oh well, there was a first time for everything. Ignoring his insult Maggie rose to her feet, brushed the grass off her slacks, and walked toward her car.

'Goodbye, nice lady,' Mouse called out. 'Don't mind Jake, he's just having a bad day.'

Maggie turned and waved. Her arms itched and the sunlight beating down on them didn't help. She could hardly wait to get into the car and turn the air conditioner on full blast.

From behind her she could hear Crazy Jake railing on Mouse.

'I swear, woman, sometimes you just don't know when to keep your trap shut.'

'Aw, c'mon, Jake. Let's play some

music. It'll make you feel better.'

Guitar riffs and beautiful singing drifted through the thick, hot air as Maggie slid behind the wheel.

8

Tattoos and Temptations

The midday sun beat down from above as Detective Maggie Reardon drove through downtown Tucson headed for the mini-mart. What was the old saying? she wondered. Oh yes, 'Mad dogs and Englishmen go out in the midday sun.' Well, she certainly wasn't an Englishman, not with the name Maggie Reardon. And she wasn't a mad dog either, although Marty the ex might vehemently disagree. Mad maybe. More than once she'd been accused of walking around with a chip the size of the Rock of Gibraltar on her shoulder.

She was looking forward to a short visit with Carlos before getting back to the job of solving a murder. He had been her second father as far back as she could remember, then after her parents died in the car accident they'd become closer than ever. He filled the void effortlessly. Being an orphaned only child she considered him her family as well as her best friend. Carlos and Prowler the cat got closer to her than anyone else was allowed, lovers or co-workers or anyone. And she had a gut feeling that Mary Rose, the watercolor artist, might well become a new addition to her small, makeshift family. Okay, so first impressions could be deceiving but still she felt a welcoming warmth in the old woman's presence. Considering this frail woman a serious suspect in a bludgeoning just didn't compute on so many levels. She had to remind herself that *everyone* was a suspect until she sifted through the evidence and eliminated them one by one.

Could she really eliminate Mary Rose as a suspect this early on in the investigation? Sometimes the person least suspect ends up being the perpetrator. But she was hard put to think of a motive. There were times when there was no motive. Juries loved to have a motive to sink their teeth into, but frequently the motive in a warped mind never surfaced. At those times forensics told all that needed to be told. The *why* didn't really matter one iota.

Maggie pulled up in front of the mini-mart and went inside.

Carlos's face lit up like a lighthouse in the darkness when he saw her enter the store. He walked around the counter and they hugged like friends who hadn't seen each other in a long time.

'I miss you, my Maggie.'

'And you, Carlos.'

'Today you stay away from the candy counter,' he said. 'I made for you a little surprise.'

'A surprise for me? Gee, and it isn't even my birthday,' she said.

He walked back around to the cash register and reached below the counter, lifting up a brown paper bag and handing it to her.

'What, no ribbon?' she said.

'Every day you come in and fill up with caffeine and sugar and every day I worry for you.'

He smiled as she peered into the bag.

'When I was a little *nino* my *mamacita* made for me every day a very special sandwich. Today I make one for you. It will grow you big and strong like me,' he laughed.

'What's in it? No *lingua* or brains I hope.'

'Boiled and sliced chayote squash with mayonnaise and onions. And good, toasted, whole wheat bread. Is very good for you.'

Maggie unwrapped the sandwich and cautiously took a bite, letting the subtle flavors dance across her taste buds.

'Carlos, this is *magnifico*. I think you missed your calling. If you opened a restaurant, I would be your first customer.'

He smiled, pleased.

★ ★ ★

Maggie drove up Ironwood Ridge, still surprised that Rocco La Crosse lived up here. She was even more surprised that he had to furnish her with a code that would allow her entrance into the gated community. He was full of surprises, that one. His address told her he was one artist that wasn't starving. He seemed to break *all* the rules. It was difficult to get a handle on him and she didn't like that — she prided herself in her ability to see through people. He was as opaque as milk glass. She hung a left and came to a stop at the entrance. She reached out the car window and punched in the security code, then watched impatiently as the huge, wrought iron gate slowly opened, allowing her entry.

The early afternoon sun half blinded her as she wove through the cobweb of streets. In her hand she held the directions she had scribbled hastily onto her notepad. Each house she passed was more magnificent than the last. The smallest one probably went for half a million, with the prices climbing from there, depending on size and view and probably the size of the pool. She ascended the driveway to a large, two-story pseudo-colonial Spanish estate, turned off the ignition, and shoved her notepad into her briefcase. She reached in and grabbed her breath mints, tossing two into her mouth. She didn't want the aroma of raw onions from Carlos's sandwich assaulting anyone. Well, not anyone, really. Rocco. She caught her trend of thought, nipped it in the bud, and mentally kicked herself. It was time to put on her best detective hat.

She had work to do.

As she slammed the car door behind her she saw Rocco come out the front door to greet her. He wore a smile as big as his girth as he welcomed her.

'I hope you found me without too much trouble,' he said. 'I'm a little tucked away from it all up here.'

'Your directions were perfect.'

As they walked up the drive Maggie looked at the metal sculptures scattered among the saguaros in the front yard and along the walkway that led to the house. The double front door was obviously a Mexican antique, two stories high, heavy and impressive. She could only wonder what was beyond the entrance. It took a minute for her eyes to adjust to the change in light as they went inside. He ushered her across the terra cotta tiled floor into a large room. One wall was covered with bookshelves. She glanced at the book spines looking for a clue to the man. Renaissance was the word that came to mind. No politics. No science fiction. But there was a leather bound collection of Mark Twain, history books ranging from ancient Greece to the American Southwest, and poetry, as well as a stack of contemporary novels by Michael Connelly, Dave Zeltserman, and Walter Mosely. And she thought she was the only one who'd discovered Zeltserman. A large book on desert flora and fauna rested beside a stack of well-worn western paperbacks by Ed Gorman. If Rocco La Crosse actually read them all, she had to conclude he was well-read and versatile. Poetry to pulp and everything in between.

A tall river rock fireplace loomed in the far corner. The furniture was leather but as unassuming as the man himself. Quality but not flashy. Masculine but tasteful. They sat across from each other in comfortable leather easy chairs. She looked directly into his eyes.

'I just wanted to ask you a few questions,' she said as she pulled out her notepad and pen from her briefcase. 'Anything that comes to mind would be helpful.'

'Ask away,' he said. 'But before we get started, would you like some coffee or something?'

'Thanks, but no. I just had lunch.'

'I guess it's down to business then. Shoot.'

'Did you notice anything out of the ordinary at the gallery the other night? Anything that may have caught your eye as unusual? Anyone who appeared out of place?'

Rocco exhaled. As Maggie waited for him to break the silence she looked around the room. In an alcove was what had to be his ultimate sculpture. A naked man and woman intertwined, with the same amusing details that had caught her eye in the gallery.

'It was busy,' Rocco said. 'People were wandering in and out all evening. Most of the faces were familiar, but there's always a few new ones. Mostly one-timers that never show up again. Absolutely nothing I can think of that would raise a red flag. Mosaic just isn't the kind of place where this sort of thing happens. I still find it hard to believe that Armando was murdered.'

'But you have reason to dislike him. Why don't you tell me about your relationship with Barbara Atwell.'

'She's my friend. We've been friends for a long time.'

'And lovers?'

'That was a long time ago,' he said.

'Until Armando Salazar came along?'

'That certainly ended it where I was concerned. But don't misunderstand. Our physical relationship was just that. Neither one of us saw it as more. It just added another dimension to a good friendship, that's all.'

'And it continued after she married Armando?' So far, his attitude seemed to match up with the statements Mary Rose had given her but she had to dig deeper. 'You remained lovers?'

'I don't think that would have been fair to anyone concerned. Emotional drama is the last thing I want in my life, believe me. Life is complicated enough. When it was over, it was over. And it was easy for us to segue back to our original friendship.'

'Easy for Barbara too?'

'She had the love of her life as well as a good friend. It was the best of both worlds.'

'And how did Adrian Velikson see it?'

A look of guarded skepticism clouded Rocco's expression. He shifted his weight and wouldn't look her in the eyes.

'I don't get where you're going,' he finally said.

'Weren't she and Barbara also lovers?'

He looked around, then lowered his voice to a near whisper. 'They were soul mates and they always will be. Some bonds are stronger than any distraction, be it lovers or marriages or whatever life tries to throw in the way. I see nothing wrong with that, do you?'

'So, you'd say that Adrian was jealous?'

'Hurt. But jealous or bent on revenge? Emphatically no. It isn't her style.'

'It would bother me. And how did she

feel about having you in the picture?'

'I feel really bad about that. Call me naive, but it was a while before I figured out their relationship. Both of them are dear to me, but once I knew about Adrian and her feelings it changed the whole dynamic for me. I'd had no idea the pain it was causing Adrian. Because of that I was ready to end things, even before Armando entered the picture.'

'Adrian must have hated you.'

'Surprisingly, no. It's complicated but let me try to explain. Once in a while lovers came between them, but the novelty always passed and they'd end up together again. Unlike Barbara, Adrian was always faithful, but Barbara's attention could wander. Adrian knew it would pass. And it always did, until Armando came along. This time Barbara made the lover her husband. Sure, Adrian was hurt but she stood back and bade her time. She knew that eventually things would return to the way they were. She wasn't comfortable being the lover on the side, but she accepted it.'

'Or maybe helped things along by

eliminating the competition?'

'I know her better than that.'

Maggie heard footsteps clipping across the tiled hallway and turned. She had assumed that the two of them were alone in the house. Barbara Atwell entered the room, wearing a bathrobe and no make-up and gripping a coffee mug like it was a lifeline. Her eyes were red and puffy, as though she'd just woken up or had been crying. Maggie guessed the later. She was the grieving widow after all. But what was she doing here in Rocco's house? He had just told her that there was nothing between them but it was obvious by her wardrobe that she'd spent the night. That made him a liar. She guessed now that the woman was available, she was fair game again. Nothing like some good, old-fashioned consolation to ease the pain. She imagined him wrapping those tattooed arms around Barbara, dishing out the solace like nobody's business.

Maggie felt a slight pang of jealousy.

'I thought I heard voices,' Barbara said with a yawn. 'Detective Reardon, what brings you here?'

Any thoughts Maggie had of a private talk with Rocco La Crosse flew out the door.

'Hello, Mrs. Atwell,' she said. 'How are you holding up?'

'As well as one could expect under the circumstances, I suppose. And call me Barbara. *Mrs.* Atwell, I'm not. And Mrs. Salazar, I wasn't. I told you I never took his name when we married, don't you remember?'

Boy, was she testy. 'Right,' was all Maggie could think to say. It struck her as an odd thing to be defensive about. So she never took his name, so what? Why make a point of it? She supposed a feminist attitude would be that in taking a husband's name one loses any semblance of their own identity. Okay, makes sense to me, she thought. Her identity is important to her.

'Do you have any suspects yet?' Barbara Atwell asked, changing the subject.

'I'm working on it.'

'I want this resolved!' She burst into

tears and left the room.

Rocco furrowed his brow and half rose from his chair, debating whether to follow Barbara out of the room. Then, after a lightning quick debate with himself, sat down again.

'You'll have to forgive her,' he said. 'She's still having a hard time dealing with this whole mess.'

'Understandable,' said Maggie as she rose. 'I might have more questions for you another time.' She looked around the room as she fished her keys from her purse.

'Your home is impressive,' she said. 'I can see you've been very successful with your art. I understand that's a rarity. Kind of like being an actor or a writer or anything else that reeks of creativity and imagination.'

Rocco laughed aloud as he rose from his chair.

'Creativity is under-appreciated and under-compensated, for sure. If you think I got all this playing with my metal and blow-torches, you're sorely mistaken. I'm definitely not the exception to the rule.'

'How so?' she asked. 'Please don't tell me you're a big-time drug lord on the side.'

He laughed even louder. 'No, nothing as exciting as that I'm afraid.' He lowered his voice and added: 'Don't spread the word Detective Reardon, but truth be known, I'm what's so lovingly referred to as a trust-fund baby.'

'Seriously?'

'We all have our cross to bear,' he said with a wink.

La Crosse. Of course. That's where she'd heard that name before. The La Crosses were one of the original families that settled the area. They'd first cashed in on the mining fever, not by digging in the dirt, but by furnishing supplies to the hordes inflicted with gold fever. And they spread out from there with a Midas touch, everything they touched turning to money and adding to their fortunes.

Mr. Rocco La Crosse was loaded and then some.

'Let me walk you to your car,' he offered.

When they approached her car, he

touched her arm, shooting little darts of electricity through her. She couldn't help but find herself attracted to him.

'As long as you're here, could I ask a favor?'

'What's that?' she asked.

'I really don't think Barbara should be behind the wheel of anything right now. My motorcycle is ready to be picked up at Victory and I've been trying to figure out how to juggle transportation so I can pick it up without leaving something behind in its place.'

'So . . . ?'

'Normally I wouldn't ask, but would you mind giving me a ride?'

'Do I look like a taxi?'

'It never hurts to ask, right?'

Maggie thought, but it didn't take much time to change her mind.

'Get in,' she said, motioning to the passenger door.

'Thanks,' he said. 'It's just off Speedway, but it's tricky to find.'

'I know right where it is,' she said.

As he slid into the seat next to her, she could detect the faint smell of men's cologne. The scent was unassuming and familiar. The guy could afford to spoil himself with the hundred dollar a bottle stuff but he was wearing Old Spice, and not too much of it either. He rode a motorcycle and drove an old beater, although he could probably afford a Maserati. It would appear that the only self-indulgence he afforded himself was his beautiful home.

And maybe Barbara Atwell.

They small-talked as she drove. She was still trying to figure him out as she hung a left just after the freeway, turned onto Anita Avenue, and pulled up in front of Arizona Victory.

Rocco La Crosse opened the car door and exited, then leaned back inside.

'Thanks again for the ride, Detective Reardon. You really saved the day.'

'It was on my way.'

He cleared his throat. 'One more thing.'

'What?'

'I was just thinking, maybe we could get together for a cup of coffee sometime.'

'That would be ill-advised,' Maggie

said, stumbling over her words. 'I'm in the middle of an ongoing investigation and . . . '

She could see the disappointment in his eyes and hoped he couldn't see what was in hers.

'Hey, it never hurts to ask,' he said.

She watched as he walked away and through the glass doors to retrieve his motorcycle.

9

Prime Suspect

It was mid-afternoon and Maggie Reardon was still thinking about Rocco La Crosse when she pulled up in front of the run-down apartment building on the south side. It was quite the contrast to the palatial home she had been in just an hour earlier. She could feel the bass from the blasting boom box even before she heard the offensive lyrics. She walked towards the steps and passed an exterior wall decorated with graffiti and Spanish cuss words. *Call Juanita for a good time* was scrawled in DayGlo orange spray paint. Some things never changed. A group of rough-looking teenagers were scattered like cockroaches on the front steps, smoking cigarettes and flashing their gang signs as they swayed to the music. If you could call it music. The lyrics were spat out rather than sung, angry and hostile, like the looks on their sullen faces. They wore the kind of expressions you'd like to slap into the next county. If the children are our future we're in deep trouble, she thought as she tried to push past them.

They stood their ground, blocking the steps and inundating her with cat calls and the sound of noisy, obscene kisses.

'Come here baby,' a young blaxican chided, motioning to his side with a slap on his hip.

'You'd best step aside,' Maggie said calmly.

'What's your hurry, *chiquita*?' asked another. He couldn't have been more than fifteen, but his grin exposed a serious case of meth-mouth, half his teeth already rotted or missing.

'You think you too good for us, *gringa*? I don't think so.'

Like a pack of hungry coyotes, they formed a circle around her, one of them giving her a shove and spinning her around.

'You gotta pay admission to go inside,' said the white kid of the group. 'Maybe that necklace around your scrawny white neck.'

He reached over and pulled the chain from where it hung under her shirt. The police badge on the end of the chain glistened in the sunlight.

'Holy mother of God,' he said as he crossed himself and took two steps backwards, nearly losing his balance in the process.

'She's a cop!'

'How was I to know?'

'No harm, *no problema, sí*?' said one of the youths as he motioned her in the direction of the doorway. At least he had the sense to attempt diffusing the situation. One by one they stepped back, clearing the path for her.

'No harm?' Maggie said. 'I oughtta haul in all your sorry asses. Assault and battery on a cop was pretty stupid, don't you think?'

'Hey, how should we know? You ain't got no uniform or nothing.'

'Our apologies,' the diffuser said, his eyes darting around nervously as he mumbled incoherently in a mixture of

Spanish and English. '*Mucho* sorry.'

'How many of you punks have warrants? Think maybe I should check?'

One by one they began to slither away.

The music was still blasting as she reached the top step. She looked down at the offending boom box, gave it a hard kick and sent it flying down the stairs. When it hit the cement the plastic shattered, sending pieces flying and the remaining punks scurrying.

Maggie welcomed the quiet.

Ordinarily she'd have taken them to the station just to teach them a lesson, but she figured they were slow learners and hardly worth the effort.

Besides, she had more important business.

The hallway smelled like last week's rotting cilantro mixed with a hint of Middle Eastern curry. Latin music wafted under the doors and into the hallway. So much for peace and quiet. Babies cried and children screamed behind closed doors. Adults were trying to be heard over the salsa beat as they yelled undecipherable profanities at each other. This end of town was like crossing the border into another country. Several countries, judging by the cooking aromas that filled the hallway. The foul aromas followed her as she walked along, seeking apartment number five. She'd smelled worse. She'd seen worse.

She knocked on the door.

It was time to pay Adrian Velikson a visit.

'You were the cop at the gallery,' Adrian said, opening the door. 'Come on in.'

'You have quite the welcoming committee out there,' said Maggie.

'Oh, them? I knocked one of them on his butt my first week here. They haven't bothered me since. They're about as dangerous as a pack of wild dogs with no teeth.'

'You think? Just give them a year or two and they'll be stabbing you for sport.'

Maggie sat down her briefcase and the two of them sat on a futon, the only piece of furniture in a room the size of a shoe box. A stove and sink below a makeshift cupboard stood against the back wall and an open door led to a small bathroom. A wooden TV tray served as an end table as well as the formal dining room. That was it. The entire apartment was the size of a closet. Adrian's bulky form filled the remaining space. It was claustrophobic. Mustard yellow walls were unadorned except for a framed photograph that hung above the futon.

Maggie looked at the lovingly framed picture. Two college girls wearing University of Arizona sweatshirts stood with their arms wrapped around each other, smiling. A younger, even more beautiful Barbara Atwell, and a thinner Adrian.

They looked content.

'Happier days?' she asked.

'They don't get any happier.'

'Why don't you give me your spin on Armando Salazar.'

'I wasn't fond of him.'

'I've gathered as much.'

'I'm probably not the person you want to ask. I'm sure my perception of the man is clouded by my personal feelings.'

'Feelings that might want to see him out of the picture?'

152

'Since day one.'

'Let's just get to the point here, Adrian. Did you murder Armando Salazar?'

Adrian laughed, but it was a sad laugh. Tears welled in her eyes.

'Did you?' asked Maggie.

'I wouldn't kill a mouse, let alone a rat like Armando.'

'You had every reason.'

'It's obvious by your questions that you're already aware of my relationship with Barbara, but I can assure you that your conclusions are wrong.'

'Why is that?'

'Barbara and I have been lovers since college. Every once in a while she strays to *the other side*. I stand back and wait for the novelty to pass, because she always comes back to me where she belongs. It's just the way it is and if that's what I have to do to keep her, well . . . '

'But she never *married* one of them before, did she?'

'No, never. But it wasn't her fault. He blinded her with his charm and she fell for it hook, line and sinker. It hurt, but I knew eventually she'd see the light and

153

things would go back the way they were. The way they were meant to be. They always have.'

'Did you live with her before then? Before Armando entered the picture?'

'For years. But I moved out before they got married. I thought I'd just be in this little place a month or two, but . . . '

'It would appear she was in the marriage for the long haul,' said Maggie, pouring salt on the wound. 'She must have loved him very much to have turned away from you.'

'Again, you're wrong.' Adrian took a breath and wiped her hand across her eyes. 'Most things between us never changed. We were still lovers, that never stopped. I never liked having to share her but it was better than nothing.'

'Was Armando aware that you two were still lovers?'

'Sure. He had his own peccadilloes.'

'If he was the chaser everyone says he was, why did he want to marry her?'

'That's the mystery. It was like he came from nowhere and swooped right in. I don't think even Barbara knows who he is,' she corrected herself, 'was, really. I told her she should check up on him, find out who he was and where he came from. She didn't want to know. As I said, she was blinded.'

'You're telling me how close you two are, yet Barbara is camped out with Rocco La Crosse instead of here with you. Why do you figure that is?'

'Look around you, detective. There's hardly room enough here for me let alone Barbara and all her things. We'll be together at the gallery as soon as you rip that tape down. In the meantime, Rocco will take good care of her.'

'Oh, I'm sure he will.' Maggie rose from the futon. 'I might want to talk with you again,' she said as she headed for the door.

Unlike most homes she visited, Adrian's surroundings revealed little to Maggie about the woman. It was as though Barbara was her entire life. Her only reason for existence. She just sat patiently in her dingy little waiting room for her wayward lover's return. Nothing more. Just the photograph on the wall, her shrine to her lover. Her obsession. It was sad really.

She admired the woman's dedication, Maggie had never loved anyone like Adrian loved Barbara, but her tenacity just reinforced Maggie's suspicions.

Adrian Velikson remained her number one suspect.

★ ★ ★

Maggie sat inside The Mosaic Gallery and looked around the room. She was trying to visualize the scenario that might have lead to Armando's death, but came up blank. Her eyes drifted to the tall shelf that had displayed his Mexican statues. The tacky statues that had created hard feelings among the *real* artists. Something caught her eye as beams of late afternoon sun washed across the floor. Something beneath the bottom shelf. She walked over and knelt by the shelves. Underneath, she spotted pieces of broken clay nestled in a thin sifting of soft white powder.

It was something that forensics had missed.

Maggie rose and looked around the room, then opened a small door that lead to a utility closet and found what she was looking for. A whisk broom and dust pan. She pulled a plastic evidence bag from her briefcase and returned to the shelf. Her knees ached and popped as she squatted down and swept the pieces into the bag.

* * *

'The autopsy's completed,' said the coroner, a small woman with a stern face. 'I'm working on my report. Two hard blows to the back of his head did the deed.'

'No big surprise there,' said Maggie. 'I just have to figure out who was holding the weapon, whatever it was.'

'He was one handsome corpse,' the coroner said, matter-of-factly. 'Makes me wonder what he must have looked like when he was breathing.'

'He must've been a looker, that's for sure.'

'And I picked several small pieces of

broken red clay from his scalp.'

'Like this?' Maggie asked, holding up the evidence bag.

The coroner squinted at the bag and nodded. 'Looks like the same stuff to me. Now if you'll excuse me, I need to finish up that report.'

'And I need to get this to forensics. Thanks again,' she said as she headed out of the icy cold room and back into the stifling heat.

* * *

Maggie Reardon sat at her desk in the police department, scouring through her notes and writing up the day's report. It had been interesting to say the least, but she still hadn't zeroed in on anything she could really sink her teeth into. And there were several people she still needed to talk to.

Tomorrow promised to be busier than today.

She wanted it wrapped up and she wanted it solved. The sooner the better.

Her cell phone rang. Caller ID told her

it was Marty the ex.

Marty the ex who didn't want to be an ex anymore.

She didn't want to answer.

But it just kept ringing, nagging her until she finally picked up.

'What,' she said, impatience in her voice.

'I've been trying to track you down all day,' he began.

'I've been busy. I've got a job, remember?'

'I don't think you'd ever let me forget,' he said. 'Maggie, you haven't eaten yet, have you?'

Silence.

'Why don't I pick you up later and take you out for a good meal? To a nice restaurant.'

The last thing she wanted to do was put on make-up and girly clothes. Much less spend time with Marty.

'No, I don't think so. I've got too much work to do.' She was trying to be polite, but it was never easy where Marty was concerned. He was like a damn puppy just begging to be kicked.

'We can make it an early night,' he said. 'You've got to eat sooner or later.'

'Marty, Marty, Marty,' she sighed. 'You're spinning your wheels. It's over.'

'That's not the impression I got the other night.'

'Impressions can be deceiving,' she said and disconnected him.

'Trouble in paradise?' said a voice from behind her.

Jerry Montana was walking toward her with a big, cocky grin and the same young rookie from the other morning following in his wake.

'None of your damn business,' she said.

He ignored her and kept on talking.

'You got that gallery murder solved yet?'

'I wasn't aware that you were my boss or that I had to answer to you.'

She returned her attention to the papers scattered across her desk.

'Don't be so touchy, Irish,' Jerry said. 'I was just wondering if you've made any progress.'

'I'm working on it,' she said, looking up and eying the rookie who stood behind him.

160

'It seems hardly worth the effort to me,' Jerry said.

'What does that mean?'

'C'mon, Irish. The guy's probably just one more illegal. One less ain't no big deal.'

Maggie said nothing but wanted to say a lot. He was the kind of cop that should never be a cop, much less pump his poison into a rookie who was still wet behind the ears. And besides, she hadn't been able to find anything on Armando Salazar. No records of any kind. Jerry'd likely hit the nail on the head, which irritated her. But he could have been less racist in making his point. She glared at him and remained silent.

'What?' he said.

'Don't call me Irish.'

'Sorry, *Detective* Reardon, is that better? But let's face it, the guy was probably a wetback.'

Maggie exhaled. 'Your surname is Montana, so why the slur?'

'My family got here through the front door. Something else you wanted to say?' he asked, winking at the rookie.

'You have no respect for the living, Jerry, so I could hardly expect you to show any respect for the dead.'

'Am I supposed to say ouch?'

'You're supposed to leave me alone.'

'Aw, c'mon, you know you love me.'

'Save it for your wife.'

The rookie stifled his snicker when Jerry Montana gave him a dirty look.

The two members of the boys' club walked away.

I'll never be in that club, Maggie thought to herself. I don't have the right equipment. They wore an invisible sign like the one on The Little Rascals' club house: *no girls allowed*. That was fine by her. All she wanted was an even break. Making detective had been a big one, even if there were some sour feelings from the boy's club.

Maggie shoved her paperwork into the desk drawer, picked up her briefcase and headed for the door. She'd had enough crap for one day. It was nearly dark as she left the station and walked to her car.

It was even darker when she got home. She fumbled with her keys, opened the door and leaned down to pet Prowler where he stood on the other side to greet her. He didn't have the best disposition, not even for a cat, but it was better than what she had to deal with in the outside world. She flipped on the light, threw down her keys and headed for the kitchen, Prowler singing his impatient chorus as he followed at her heels.

Maggie filled his dish and headed for the shower, nearly tripping over Prowler's litter box as she stumbled into the bathroom.

The lukewarm water felt great against her skin as she washed away the day's grime. She stood under the stream for a long time, her mind replaying the day as the water got cooler and cooler. Barbara Atwell was at Rocco La Crosse's place. Adrian sat waiting in her hovel. Things were slowly beginning to add up but to what she wasn't sure. Could the three of them be in it together? And for what purpose? Her mind wandered. Rocco had smelled good sitting next to her in the car. Stop it, Maggie! She stuck her head under the stream and gave her short red hair a shampoo with her bar of body soap then rinsed it out quickly. The water had turned ice cold. How long had she been standing there? She turned it off and stepped out, grabbed a towel and dried off.

The phone was ringing.

And ringing.

She threw on her robe and walked to the front room.

Caller ID said it was Marty.

She ignored it, plopped down into her chair and turned on the remote.

Bad boys, bad boys. The theme from *Cops* was music to her ears as Prowler jumped onto her lap and they settled in for the evening.

10

Whitewashed

Detective Maggie Reardon woke up to a growling stomach, a grating infomercial, and a hungry cat. She was curled up in her living room chair, having fallen asleep in front of the television the night before. Not only had she failed to make it to the bedroom, she had forgotten to eat and she was starving.

She did her morning routines, fed the cat, gulped down her coffee, dressed and headed for the police station for her daily briefing. Her stomach growled noisily as she sat impatiently in the squad room. Jerry Montana had somehow managed a chair next to hers, his rookie trainee in the seat on the other side of him. The kid looked like he was fresh off a Wisconsin farm. Blond hair, blue eyes, and a slightly naive demeanor. The only thing missing was some straw sticking out of his mouth.

That would change, she thought, smiling to herself. The little rube was in for a surprise. Being a cop in Tucson wasn't like patrolling the streets of some hayseed farming community where there wasn't much to do besides bust an Amish for not having a taillight on the back of his buggy. He'd be facing more murders in one week here than he'd probably see in ten years in Podunk. And he certainly needed some big city training before they turned him lose. She leaned across Jerry Montana to speak with the kid.

'I never did catch your name,' she said. 'Jerry's a bit short-changed in the manners department.'

'Aaron Iverson,' he replied with a warm smile. 'My pleasure.'

'Welcome to Tucson, Aaron Iverson. Maggie Reardon. Where did you transfer from?'

'Minnesota,' he said, in an accent right out of the movie Fargo. 'Little town outside of St. Paul. Yah, I've had enough snow to last me a lifetime.'

Minnesota. Wisconsin. Not a bad guess she thought to herself.

'Tucson warm enough for you?'

'Hotter than I figured, I must admit.'

'But it's a dry heat,' said Maggie with a smirk. 'Think you can take it?'

'You betcha. As long as I don't have to break my back shoveling the sunshine.'

Maggie leaned back and returned her attention to the front of the room.

'A little young for you, don't you think?' Jerry whispered in her ear.

'Pig,' she said under her breath. Her conversation with Crazy Jake at the park flashed back. He'd referred to her as a pig. Well, pig was the perfect word for Jerry Montana, but not because of his profession.

Maggie breathed a sigh of relief when they were dismissed. The morning ritual slowed her down and she was ready to get started. Today she would pay a visit to the next person on her list. An artist named Misty Waters who'd been at the gallery the night of the reception. Maggie hoped that she could shed some light on things. So far nobody had given her any valuable information and she didn't like being in a holding pattern.

But she had to take care of something else first. She had to fill her stomach.

She pulled up in front of the nearest all-you-can-eat breakfast buffet, paid up front, and grabbed a large plate. She looked around the room at the breakfast crowd. Maggie was probably the only person in the place under sixty-five. Even if the food was lousy, it was a good place to fill up if your Social Security couldn't buy you three meals a day. Or if you were a hungry cop in a hurry.

She watched as an elderly woman wrapped a fistful of bacon into a paper napkin and shoved it into her oversized purse. It would probably serve as her lunch and dinner.

She found an empty booth, sat down and inhaled her plate of food in record time.

* * *

Maggie Reardon pulled up in front of the small white house that sat in a quiet cul-de-sac. The front yard was a blank palette. A collection of rocks with no living plants in sight, not even the usual Tucson weeds that crept up when you weren't looking. It was devoid of personality and would look abandoned were it not for the total absence of foliage. Someone spent a lot of time digging up palo verde sprouts and brittlebush and anything else that dared raise its ugly head.

She reached the front door and was ready to ring the bell when she heard voices from inside.

'Who's your daddy!' Someone was yelling in the most godawful voice she'd ever heard. 'Come on baby, who's your daddy.' She visualized some ugly little troll of a man with gnarled hands pacing the floor.

'Shut up,' said a female voice. 'Just stop it.'

'Gimme some sugar.'

'Can't you be nice? Haven't I taught you better?'

'Baby,' the creep said. 'Lay kisses on me.' Followed by a loud slurping sound. The guy sounded disgusting.

'Baretta, stop it right now.'

Well, this was certainly entertaining. Maggie wanted to listen a little longer but the verbal sparring stopped so she rang the bell. She'd have preferred talking to Misty Waters alone, but would make the best of it and hope the woman opened up to her questions.

From the other side, Maggie could hear at least three locks being unlocked.

'And I don't want one more word out of you,' Misty said before she opened the door.

'Misty Waters?' said Maggie.

'Detective Reardon? I've been expecting you,' she replied softly. 'Come in.'

Misty closed the door, bolted and locked it, then slid a chain into place before leading the detective into the room. Did she feel that unsafe, even with an armed cop in the room?

The interior was lit up brighter than a shopping mall. Every lamp in the place was burning and they weren't sixty watt bulbs. 100 watters in every corner washed their glaring light across even whiter walls. Walls filled with white paintings in white frames and a floor covered with an impractical white carpet. Floor lamps and table lamps, all with white shades. Recessed lighting. The place looked like the inside of a lighting fixture store in Alaska. She'd never seen so many lights, not even on a house gaudily decorated for the holidays.

'Ooh, hot mama.' Maggie turned in the direction of his scratchy voice, ready to tell him to can it. Off in a far corner stood a tall birdcage. Inside a white cockatoo was dancing from one foot to the other and she could have sworn he was laughing.

'Shut up, Baretta,' said Misty. 'I'm sorry. His previous owner thought it was cute to teach him filthy words. If only I'd know what I was in for.' An embarrassed blush stood out against the sickly pallor of her skin. 'I've been trying to retrain him.'

'I'd say your work's cut out for you.'

Maggie took out her notepad and pen. 'I wanted to ask you a few questions about Armando Salazar.'

'From the gallery? Is he in some kind of trouble?' Maggie detected relief in her eyes, as though she'd been expecting something else entirely. Misty appeared to be in her mid-twenties and Maggie looked at her pure white hair for a hint of darker roots. Could a person actually bleach their hair that white? It couldn't possibly be natural. Not on a woman that young.

'I might as well cut to the chase and save you some time. He's been murdered.'

'How awful,' she said with no hint of emotion.

'Did you know him well?'

'Oh, no. I don't know anyone well.'

'Why is that?'

'That's how I prefer it. I like being left alone. When one gets too close . . . ' Her words drifted off as well as her attention.

'If I could ask you a few questions,' said Maggie.

'I can't see how I can possibly be of help to you, Detective Reardon. I know a few names from the gallery, but that's all. I only go because it's expected of me. I don't entangle myself in their personal lives.'

Maggie Reardon had seen plenty of odd birds in her life but never one as bland and guarded as Misty Waters. It was strange to say the least. She asked the artist several questions and each was answered either with a shrug or a blank look. It appeared that she knew nothing about any of them and Maggie suspected they knew even less about her.

Continuing the conversation was useless.

She'd batted zero.

'Before I leave I'd like your prints,' she said, indicating the kit at her side.

'Am I a suspect?'

'No.'

'Then come back with a warrant.'

Curious reaction, Maggie thought.

'Thank you for your time. If I have any more questions, I'll call you. In the meantime, here's my card. Feel free to call me if you can think of anything that might be helpful.'

As Maggie left she could hear the locks sliding into place as the door closed behind her.

Back at the station, Maggie sat in front of the computer at her desk. She was having no luck pulling up information on Misty Waters. The name came up nowhere, not even on a driver's license. It was as if the elusive Misty Waters didn't exist. What was she hiding? Maggie suspected she'd have found a hit of some kind if the woman had consented to be printed. But getting a warrant would be impossible without some concrete evidence. And there was none. Just her cop's gut instinct that Misty was hiding something. And that would never wash with a judge.

It was as if the woman was nonexistent.

She decided to put Misty Waters on the back burner for the moment and move forward.

She headed out the door and walked to her car. A soft veil of smoke from the distant fires blurred the outline of the surrounding mountains and the ground was hot beneath her feet. Tucson needed monsoon now more than ever. It would help put out the fires as well as provide relief from the sweltering temperatures. But there wasn't a cloud to be seen in the hazy skies. Tempers rose with the temperatures and made the city a rumbling volcano ready to explode. Everyone needed a break, Maggie most of all.

Where were the rain dancers when you needed them?

Maggie threw the car into gear and headed to the gallery.

When she arrived she sat in front in her car, looking at the gallery, wondering what had inspired the attack on Armando Salazar. She wanted to put the pieces together as neatly as the chipped and broken tiles on the entryway arch. And she would.

Once out of the car, Maggie went about the task of pulling down the streamers of yellow tape that had wrapped the gallery like a birthday present. Everyone she had questioned had been in agreement on one thing. This wasn't the kind of place where one would expect something like a murder to occur.

Maggie sat beneath the shade of the

palo verde tree in the side yard. The place where Barbara Atwell and Adrian Velikson sat the morning the body was discovered. As well as Rocco La Crosse. It was peaceful and serene and Maggie felt more relaxed than she had in a long time. She sat for a few minutes, absorbing the welcome silence.

Okay, enough goofing off, she told herself.

Time to get to work.

She walked back to the car, opened the doors, and threw the bundles of yellow crime scene tape onto the floor of the back seat. It was time to be the bearer of some good news.

She headed west, the early afternoon sun shining in her face. God, what she'd give for some overcast to dim the glare. Halfway up the hill she hung a left and punched in Rocco La Crosse's security code and waited while the gate opened. She drove up the winding streets and pulled up in front of his house.

Her heart skipped like a teenager when she rang the bell. She was anticipating Rocco's welcome, but when the door opened Barbara Atwell stood there. She had traded her bathrobe for some real clothes and her eyes were no longer bloodshot. An improvement since their last encounter.

'I'd like to speak with Rocco,' she said.

'He's not here. Is there something I can do for you?'

'As long as I'm here, I have a few questions.'

'I thought I already answered them,' she said. 'But okay, come on in.'

The two women sat across from each other in the bookcase-lined room, Barbara with her back straight and her demeanor composed. She wore a hint of makeup and her blonde hair was pulled into a tidy bun at the nape of her neck.

'Where did you meet Armando?'

'Let me think,' she said. 'Oh, it was at a fundraiser for the women's shelter. It seems like a lifetime ago now. Almost like a dream. I remember thinking how impressed I was to see so many men giving their support for battered women. After all, it was husbands and boyfriends who were responsible for their dilemma in the first place.'

'Go on.'

'There were probably ten or fifteen men there. Rocco had donated one of his works for the raffle, as did several of the artists from the gallery. He's always been more than generous. In so many ways. We raised a lot of money that night.'

'And?'

'I remember I was looking around the room. Armando was standing by a far table holding court with a group of fawning females. When he looked over I was drawn like a magnet. I crossed the room and introduced myself. We were inseparable from that moment on.' Barbara exhaled a long, weary sigh.

She must have caught the skepticism in Maggie's eye. 'Believe me, if you could have seen him alive, you'd understand. He was irresistible.'

'Have you contacted his family?'

'His family?'

'He must have some relatives.'

'He never talked about family.'

'Is he from here?'

'I don't know. It never came up.'

'You said he made frequent trip to Nogales. Do you think . . . ?'

'I really have no idea, Detective Reardon. He never volunteered and I never asked.'

Barbara Atwell shifted her weight uncomfortably in her chair.

Who would marry someone knowing nothing about them? Either this woman had been a love struck fool, as her friend Adrian had suggested, or she knew more about her dearly departed Armando than she was willing to share.

Maggie rose and thanked Barbara for her time.

'I still have a few questions for Rocco. Where could I find him?'

'He's out at the museum today.'

'The museum?'

Barbara looked at her like she was stupid.

'There's a lot of museums in Tucson,' said Maggie.

'The Arizona Sonoran Desert Museum,' she said, as if it were the only museum in town. 'He volunteers a couple of days a week.'

'Volunteers?'

'He's a docent. He gives tours, handles animals, gives the occasional lecture.'

One more surprise from Mr. Rocco La Crosse, thought Maggie. 'Interesting,' she said.

'He believes in giving back to the community.'

Maggie reached into her pocket and handed Barbara the gallery keys. 'Forensics has finished and the crime scene tape is down. You can go back.' Unless you want to spend some more time rolling around here with Rocco, she thought.

Barbara looked at the keys in her hand. 'That's the first good news I've had.'

'You might want to give Adrian Velikson a call,' she said with a wink as she walked out the door.

*　*　*

Detective Maggie Reardon drove through the imposing wrought iron gate and headed down the hill. She hung a right at

180

Painted Hills and sped along at twenty over the limit. When she reached Speedway she hung a right and headed back up the hill to Gates Pass and toward the Arizona Sonoran Desert Museum. She passed the International Wildlife Museum on her right and sped up. Funny, she'd been born and raised in Tucson and had never set foot in either one of them. It was like being in Orlando without ever having gone to Disney World. Well, she finally found an excuse to visit at least one of them.

And her excuse was Rocco La Crosse.

Surely he held the key to something. He had to be knee deep in the Mosaic Gallery murder mystery. Was that her reason for paying him another visit?

She squinted her eyes against the afternoon sun and told the butterflies in her stomach to knock it off.

11

The Snake Charmer

When the somber looking woman at the museum gate told Detective Maggie Reardon the entrance fee, she cringed slightly at the ticket price, then flashed her badge.

'I'm not here for a tour. I need to speak with Rocco La Crosse,' she said.

The woman gave her a skeptical frown, then waved her through. Being a cop was a double-edged sword. The badge always opened the door, but she'd be welcomed with about as much warmth as an enemy on someone's native soil. People avoided eye contact, or ran like rabbits if they were up to no good. But let somebody be on the victim's side of trouble and they were sure glad to see her. It amused her. And it ticked her off.

'Excuse me,' Maggie said, 'but where exactly would I find him?'

'Just a minute,' the woman said, thumbing through her schedule and running her finger down the page. 'Okay, La Crosse. He's with the reptiles and invertebrates. You might want to hurry. He's probably finishing up by now.'

'Where exactly?'

'Go through the turnstiles and turn right. It's the first building.'

Reptiles, Maggie thought as she pushed through the turnstile and entered the building. A house full of snakes. Charming. The cool air hit her like an arctic breeze as she walked into the semi-darkness and adjusted her vision. She stood at the rear of a group of nine people who were listening intently as Rocco La Crosse spoke. He wore a white dress shirt with a Desert Museum insignia on the sleeve and tan khaki pants. Unlike the scruffy fellow she first saw at the gallery, or the relaxed man surrounded by his books, today he wore an aura of professionalism and looked neat as a pin. Just how many people is he? she wondered. The artist, the sculptor, the reader, the biker, the trust-fund baby, the tattoo freak. Barbara Atwell's lover? The murderer? How many hats does this guy wear? He was like one of the chameleons in the reptile aquarium behind where he stood. Every time she saw him he revealed another layer cloaked in another shade of mystery.

Today she watched him capture his audience with the authority of someone who would know the answers to any question they might ask.

In his hands Rocco held a large snake that coiled itself around his wrist and lower arm. The group *oohed* and *aahed* as its tongue flicked in and out of its mouth. Rocco smiled at their reactions and continued speaking.

'As you can see, this desert king snake is identifiable by its black color and thin cream colored bands, although there are also several other varieties native to this area.'

'What does he eat?' asked a little boy.

'He's gonna eat you,' teased another who must have been his older brother.

'Is not.'

'He has a healthy appetite,' Rocco

continued. 'He likes to eat rodents and other snakes, so if you find one in your yard you probably won't have a problem with pack rats or mice or ground squirrels. They're his breakfast, lunch, and dinner.'

'A snake that eats other snakes? I'll bet he can't eat a rattlesnake. They're poisonous,' said big brother.

'There are no poisonous snakes,' said Rocco.

'Are too!'

'No, snakes are venomous, not poisonous. They have venom. But the king snake is immune to a rattlesnake's venom, so the answer is yes. A king snake can kill a rattler. And eat him too.'

'Is he vem, vem-inous too?' asked the little brother.

'No, he ain't,' said big brother. 'Can't you see he's holding it? Do you see him getting bit? I bet you could pick one up in our yard and pet it.'

Rocco laughed. 'I wouldn't recommend it. This one is used to people holding it, but in the wild he'd protect himself. And he's got lots and lots of sharp teeth.'

'You think you're such a big know-it-all,' the boy said to his big brother.

The mother nudged them both. 'Shhh.' she said, 'behave yourselves.'

Rocco looked around the room. When he spotted Maggie standing at the rear he smiled.

She nodded.

'That about wraps it up,' he said. 'Are there any more questions?'

'I was wondering how old the snake is and how long they live,' said an elderly gentleman with an east coast accent. His wife stood uncomfortably at his side, holding on to him as if the snake could sprout wings and fly across the room.

'I don't know how old this particular snake is,' said Rocco, 'but we have an old gopher snake that's been here over twenty-two years.'

Rocco got a mischievous twinkle in his eye. 'Before we move on, who would like to come up here and pet him?'

'Not me,' said the elderly woman with a shudder.

'No way,' said the little boy.

'Chicken,' said his brother.

'Well, I'll bet you won't either.'

And he didn't.

There were no takers, but who could blame them? People have had an aversion to snakes since the Garden of Eden.

Again Rocco's eyes went to the back of the room. He gestured to Maggie.

'How about you, young lady? I'll bet you'd like to come up here to pet my friend.'

'Me?'

'Sure, come on up. I promise he won't bite.'

Maggie showed no hesitation as she walked up and stood next to Rocco La Crosse. She was the big, bad cop and she had no intention of weakening her image. She reached over and ran her hand down the length of the snake never looking away from Rocco's face. He looked impressed as she pet it. Just the reaction she wanted.

The small crowd gasped in unison.

'So, what do you think?'

'I'm surprised. I expected it to be . . . slimy.'

'Anyone else as brave as this fearless woman?'

'Me. I am!' said the little boy, rushing up.

Maggie stood off to the side as he reached over, hesitated, then touched the snake.

'Ha ha, I'm braver than you are,' he said to his brother. 'Now who's the chicken?'

People applauded, then one by one, walked out of the building and into the heat.

Only Maggie Reardon, Rocco La Crosse, and the king snake remained.

'Let me put my friend away and I'll be right back,' he said. 'Wait here.'

So she waited, enjoying the cool air and looking at the snakes and lizards and other creatures housed safely behind their glass enclosures.

Maggie turned at the sound of the familiar voice behind her.

'I was beginning to think our paths might never cross again,' Rocco said. 'That would be a shame. Are you here on business or for pleasure?'

'I'm always strictly business, Mr. La Crosse.'

'All's the pity.'

'Is there somewhere we can talk?'

'Let's take the scenic route,' he said. 'Unless you're in a hurry.'

'I've got a few minutes.'

The two of them walked along a meandering pathway, surrounded by native desert foliage. Each tree and bush had a placard identifying its species. And what information wasn't on the sign Rocco filled in for her. She was impressed by his knowledge although he kept testing her, just like he had done with the snake.

'This one is edible,' he said. 'And the local tribes grind it up to a powder and use it in cooking like we use flour.' He pulled a pod off the tree. 'Here, taste it,' he said as he handed her a small bean.

'You're kidding, right?'

'Don't worry, it's not poison.'

'Then I'm game.'

Maggie popped it into her mouth and chewed it, not sure what to expect. It wasn't bad. But it wasn't good either.

'You have a sense of adventure,' he

said, 'but I wouldn't have expected less.'
Then pointing to a bench, 'Why don't we
sit in the shade? I've been standing for
hours and I'm tired.' They sat down,
Rocco just a bit closer than she found
comfortable. She inched a little farther
away from him so that their legs wouldn't
touch. But once again, she felt that little
surge of electricity flowing through her.
She cleared her throat, trying to remember exactly why she'd deemed it necessary
to see him again.

She found him so distracting that it
took a minute to compose her thoughts.

Maybe, like him, she was testing for a
reaction.

'It's regarding the gallery. I stopped at
your place to give your house guest back
her keys. It's okay for her to go back
home. That is, if she wants to.'

'That's good news. But I wonder . . . '

'What?'

'Her husband was murdered there.
Maybe she isn't ready to face that yet. I
wouldn't be.'

It sounded as if Rocco La Crosse
would like to keep Barbara Atwell under

his roof a little longer.

'No, I'm sure it won't be easy. You're her friend, right? I'm sure you have a sense for what she can handle.'

'Right now nothing's easy for her. She's walking around like a zombie.'

'I should get going. I have an appointment with . . . ' Maggie pulled her notepad from her briefcase and checked her notes. ' . . . Belinda Blume. Wasn't she the one who bulldozed her way into the gallery the other day?'

'What can I say? Belinda is Belinda. Not the most diplomatic, for sure, but she's one mean sculptress, I'll give her that. And she'd be the first to tell you.'

'I get the impression you don't like her.'

'I can take her or leave her. She tends to verbalize anything that pops into her head. Unedited. I find honesty refreshing, but hers can be abrasive. Her insensitivity the other day was uncalled for. It was mean-spirited.'

Maggie reran the episode in her mind. Belinda acted like the most important thing was her missing sculpture and

191

Armando's death was nothing more than a minor inconvenience. She didn't know the woman but her first impression had been negative. And the woman obviously resented him. She had made no secret of that. Even in the middle of Barbara Atwell's tragedy she'd managed to get in a dig or two at Armando Salazar.

She had motive.

'Thanks for your time.'

Maggie rose, not sure where to find the exit.

'This way,' he said. She felt that same animal attraction as he held her arm and escorted her in the right direction. She'd have to watch herself or he'd steer her right into the danger zone. 'Would you like a cold drink or some hot coffee before you hit the road? There's a little café right over there.'

'No thanks, I need to get back to work,' she said.

'All work and no play?'

'That's my motto.'

'You should come back sometime and really look around. There's so much to see.'

'Is that a sales pitch?'

'I'd be more than happy to give you the grand tour.'

And what about Barbara? Maggie thought.

'I'll keep that in mind, Mr. La Crosse,' she said, trying to maintain some distance and formality to her tone.

'I hope you will, Detective Reardon.'

By the time Maggie reached her car the cell phone was ringing.

It was Marty.

She picked up.

'Marty, I'm busy here.'

'I'd like to see you.'

The guy wasn't good at taking hints. It was time to spell it out for him and end the nonsense once and for all.

'We do need to talk,' she said.

'When can I come over?'

'I think it would be better if we meet somewhere,' she said, determined not to put herself in the same position as last time. If he came over she knew exactly where they'd end up.

'I have some last minute things to wind up. How about we meet at our favorite coffee shop? Say around six?'

Silence.

When he finally spoke he said: 'I guess you're still calling the shots. Six it is.'

★　★　★

As Detective Maggie Reardon drove through heavy afternoon traffic to the east side of town the voice on the radio announced that the last of the fires was ninety percent contained. It was the best news she'd heard all week. The smoke still hugged the mountains but it would soon dissipate and the air would be clear again. Once the heat took a break things would return to normal, but there was still no hint of welcoming rain in sight.

At least things were moving in the right direction. She wished she could say the same thing for the investigation. Everyone she talked to was a suspect. Each of them had a motive to see Armando Salazar out of the picture.

Except for pot-smoking Mary Rose. As she pulled up in front of her next stop, she smiled at the memory of the pleasant visit that they'd had and determined to pay her a social call once this mess was behind her. Although colorful, Mary Rose appeared to be the only normal person in the entire menagerie of kooks from The Mosaic Gallery.

The small stucco house was hidden behind an overgrowth of creosote bushes that had reproduced in every square inch of the small front yard. They grew everywhere. Large ones and small ones reached out their scraggly arms like the triffids from the old horror movie. It gave the impression that the place was long deserted. Maggie walked up the cracked walkway wondering what answers she'd find here. Holding her briefcase in one hand and her portable fingerprint kit under her arm, Maggie Reardon knocked on Belinda Blume's door. She looked around the porch, at the broken flower pots filled with dead plants and garden gnomes covered in dust, smiling their creepy smiles. She half-expected Lurch from the Adam's Family to open the door.

'Keep it short,' said Belinda Blume as

she opened the door. Red clay stained her hands and her long denim apron and smudged across her cheek. 'I'm busy and I need to get back to work.'

The inside of the house was tidy compared to the exterior. At least the living room was. Off to the left Maggie could see a large workroom where a kiln stood in the corner. There were long wooden tables filled with sculptures and pots and glazes. Completed works stood beside works in progress. Maggie surmised that this had once been a dining room, which gave her a hint to the woman's priorities.

'When did you last see Armando Salazar?' she asked as they sat down on a green Naugahyde couch right out of nineteen seventy-five.

'The night of the reception, like everybody else.'

'Did you speak with him?'

'I ignored him. He's a jerk.'

'Was,' Maggie corrected.

'Was, and good riddance.'

Red clay.

'Why did you dislike him so much?

Everyone else seems to have found him charming.'

'He was an ass and Barbara Atwell was an ass to have catered to him. Did you know he didn't even have to pay her a commission for that crap he sold? She just let him set up those statues and pocket every cent he made from them.'

'And you resented that?'

'I resented everything about him. You can only imagine how . . . demeaning . . . it was for me to have my masterpieces in the same room with his stuff. And he didn't even create them. He just went down to Mexico and bought them by the dozens and put them on display. And the worst of it was that he managed to sell them. But that shouldn't have mattered to Barbara. There's more important things than a dollar. I mean, Mosaic always had a good reputation and I just don't get it.'

'Maybe because he was her husband and she loved him.'

Red clay.

'Give me a break. There's love and then there's business.'

Belinda shifted her weight impatiently.

'If that's all,' she said.

'Were you and Armando intimate?'

Belinda gave the detective a sarcastic smile.

'If you could call it that. Sure, when he first showed up I gave him a tumble. Nearly everyone did. But I assure you his performance was hardly worthy of an encore.'

'Nothing since then?'

'My time is too important to waste it on mediocrity. Poor Barbara, she probably never knew the difference. After all, *women* are her specialty.' She spat the words out. 'Are you done now?'

She was outspoken. She was rude. She was self-involved. Maggie bet she thought the universe revolved around her. Had she rejected Armando or had it been the other way around? That would certainly be another reason for her to feel such hostility toward him. Even as his cold body lay in the morgue she didn't miss an opportunity to trash him. Her emotions ran deeper than mere competition over a few pieces of art.

'You had a work on display that was

apparently stolen.'

'That still pisses me off, even if I am getting paid for it. I'll never know where my Gaia is or who wanted her so badly.'

'What did she look like?'

'Who?'

'Your Gaia.'

'She was beautiful, one of the best pieces I've ever created. She captured the essence of the goddess to perfection,' she said, pride and arrogance in her voice.

'I'm sure she was,' said Maggie. 'In what medium did you sculpt her?'

'Red clay.'

Red clay. Armando had shards of red clay imbedded in his scalp, Maggie thought. There were small pieces of red clay that she'd swept from underneath the shelves in the gallery. There was a good chance that Belinda Blume's statue had been the murder weapon. She wondered how she would react if she thought her masterpiece had been destroyed. Or could Belinda have used it to kill off her rival? It was certainly a possibility.

'I like your work, Belinda,' Maggie said looking into the next room. 'I'm not an art connoisseur and I live on a cop's salary but I'd love one of your pieces. Do you have something on the small and inexpensive side?'

She could see that Belinda was flattered. They walked into the adjacent room and Maggie spotted a small clay bowl. 'How much for that one?'

Belinda picked up the bowl and scrutinized it.

'It's probably out of your price range, Detective Reardon. Tell you what, you can have it, my compliments. Just let me get back to work,' she said, wiping bits of clay onto her apron. 'I'm in the middle of a project.'

'You have a generous spirit,' she lied as Belinda handed her the bowl. 'But before I go, I'd like to get your prints,' she said, indicating the kit that sat on the floor.

'You're kidding me, right?'

'We're getting everyone's prints,' she said. 'It's just a matter of elimination.'

'C'mon lady, if you think I killed that jerk you're way off base. I create, I don't destroy. Not even a cockroach like Armando Salazar.'

'I'm not accusing you, but your cooperation would be helpful.'

'If I give you my prints will you get out of here?'

'Of course, I can see your time is precious.' And I can see that you're one of the most narcissistic creatures I've ever encountered, Maggie said to herself as she opened her kit and got down to business.

It would be interesting to see just where Belinda Blume's prints showed up.

And if her hatred for Armando Salazar outweighed her love for her precious Gaia statue.

Maggie would drop off her little gift to forensics to see if the clay matched the little shards imbedded in Armando Salazar's skull.

12

Lunatic Love Song

Maggie Reardon removed her sunglasses and adjusted her eyes to the change in light as she entered the café. She looked around the room, scanning the row of cheap vinyl booths until she spotted him. Marty stood up and waved. He wore a short-sleeved shirt and a wide grin.

'Over here,' he said.

She walked over, relieved at his good mood. But he was disappointed when she sat in the booth across from him instead of scooting in next to him. Once again he was sending a silent message that she had displeased him. She was reminded again of why she wanted his negativity out of her life. She didn't want his approval much less need it. But that wasn't why she was here sitting across from the man she hoped never to see again. She wanted to mend a severely broken fence and walk away with a clear conscience.

'Sorry I'm late,' she said, reaching over and picking up a jelly-laced menu.

'I'm used to it.'

Dishes clattered and glasses pinged against each other accompanied by voices that bounced off the walls. Muzak and laughter and a chef ringing his bell and yelling, 'order's up.' The place was packed despite its offering of mediocre food. It was cheap and it was convenient and they always had an early bird special. Their mashed potatoes had the consistency of setting plaster, but they managed an edible burger, the safest choice on a sadly limited menu.

Marty watched in silence as he swirled his straw in the tall glass of iced tea he'd ordered while waiting for her. Around and around went the straw, clanking against the ice cubes until Maggie wanted to scream *stop*. She stifled the temptation. She didn't want this meeting to be confrontational but there were things that needed saying. She wasn't looking forward to it, but a little humble pie was in order if she wanted to end it amicably.

Her visit with Belinda Blume was an eye-opener. The woman's coldness had hit home. Maggie wasn't as self-serving, not by a long shot, but she knew she could have handled things better with Marty. She regretted not having considered his feelings, just her own. Even Marty deserved better than that. The ice stopped clanking as he reached in his fingers and fished the lemon slice from the glass. He held it to his mouth and sucked on it, then shuddered from its sourness.

'This is hardly the place I'd have chosen for a romantic dinner,' he said. 'And I doubt they have much of a wine list.'

His attempt at humor was a relief.

A waitress walked over, impatient to take their order.

'I'll have a burger with fries. Extra mayo on the side,' Maggie said. 'And a diet soda.'

'Same here,' said Marty. 'Just skip the mayo and the soda.' He gave Maggie a sideways glance when he said skip the mayo. Passive aggressive. Apparently mayo was out of line too. As if her dietary choices were supposed to match his own. She failed to measure up to his expectations on so many levels that she wondered why he hung on. Did he think he could break her spirit and she'd march in step? On the surface he was gentle, almost meek in his demeanor, but as she got to know him the telltale signs began to surface. They were subtle, but they always are at first. She knew where those control issues led. She'd seen the empty faces of broken women on domestic abuse calls and it was frightening.

Once they broke your spirit they started breaking your bones.

It was just a matter of time.

The silence between them was awkward and Marty again fidgeted with his straw. Maggie reached over and put her hand over his then pulled away, afraid he would misinterpret the gesture. 'I'm glad you had a change of heart,' he said. 'I know I sound like a broken record, but when we're apart I miss you. And it's not just the sex.'

The waitress returned and dropped the

dinner plates in front of them.

Maggie tore into her burger, out of avoidance more than hunger. She had to say the right thing and was trying to form the right words before she spoke. It was delicate and touchy and she wanted it right. She wasn't so hot in the diplomacy department but this was important. She slowed her eating, a lame attempt at holding off the moment. When she looked up Marty had stopped chewing and was watching as she wiped a stream of melting mayo off her chin. He had mood swings worse than a female fighting PMS. His silent agitation was gone and he looked so content that she hated to spoil things.

'This is nice,' he said. 'Not the ambience of the room, mind you, but the way we're sitting here just like an old married couple.'

Oh God.

Maggie placed her paper napkin next to her plate and took a deep breath.

'Marty, I owe you an apology . . . '

'Maggie . . . '

'No, let me speak. You need to hear me out.' She pushed the plate aside. 'We had something, just not what it should have been. When it ended I was only thinking about my feelings and never took yours into consideration. I was insensitive and I was wrong and I need to apologize for that.'

'But that's all behind us.'

'No, it's not. When you came over the other night I didn't mean to mislead you.'

'Mislead me? Everything was perfect. Until you kicked me out,' he laughed, 'but I understand. You needed your sleep.'

'Don't make excuses for me. I could have handled things better.'

His expression turned serious. 'Okay, go on.'

'You got the impression that I was picking up where we left off, but I wasn't.'

'Then what the hell was it?'

'I got caught up in the moment. It was sex. Nothing more. It shouldn't have happened, it won't happen again, and I'm sorry.'

A shadow fell over his face that gave her the chills. He was looking at her, but there was no emotion behind his eyes. It was the same coldness she'd seen in the interrogation room so many times. It was unnerving. She disliked when he looked at her with puppy dog eyes, but this was even worse. He stared at her, silent.

'It's over,' she said.

'Still calling the shots.'

There was a long pause.

'I see,' he finally said, his voice steely and controlled.

'So you understand?'

'Perfectly.'

Maggie rose to leave, then turned to face him one last time.

'I'm sorry I hurt you,' she said.

★ ★ ★

Maggie left the grocery store holding a single plastic bag filled with cat food for Prowler, canned chili for herself and a box of donuts. She was exhausted and ready to crash. She rested the bag's weight against her side holster as she headed for her car. Things had gone well with Marty. Better than she'd anticipated. She heaved a sigh, relieved that he was finally history and she could move forward. Alone. No more relationships. Her judgment was flawed. Detective Reardon was a force to be reckoned with, but Maggie the woman had a blind spot in the romance department. One way or the other the blame rested on her, whether it was her independent, abrasive attitude that scared them off or just picking the wrong guy in the first place. It was no wonder each relationship ended in disaster.

It was safer to fly solo.

Ending up as 'the eccentric old lady who lived with her cat' had definite appeal.

She slid into the front seat and turned on the ignition. The gauge read empty. She pulled out of the parking lot hoping the fumes would get her to the nearest station. She hit every red light along the way. Why couldn't the city coordinate them more efficiently? It was feeling like a conspiracy aimed directly at her as her eyes kept returning to the gas gauge. When she pulled into the gas station the car was sputtering and coughing its last gasp. She slid her credit card into the pump, punched in her zip code and lifted the nozzle. Numbers swirled like rows of fruit on a slot machine. If the price of gas goes any higher, she thought, the whole town will be walking right back to the Middle Ages.

★　★　★

The streets were dark but for neon lights that whispered and flickered like something out of an old noir movie. Storefronts closed, traffic thinned, and the voice on Detective Maggie Reardon's car radio said that within a week rain was in the forecast. Welcome rain. The smoke that had hovered over Tucson was dissipating, and a dip in the sweltering temperatures was on the way. She smiled to herself as she pulled up the drive.

As she was exiting the car her cell phone rang.

She looked at the caller ID and picked up.

'Mr. La Crosse?'

'Detective Reardon.'

'Hold on a minute,' she said. She held

the cell phone against her shoulder with her chin as she juggled her briefcase and groceries. Halfway up the sidewalk she rearranged her load. At the door she turned her key in the lock and began to push with her hip. She put the phone back to her ear.

'Sorry about that,' she said.

Someone grabbed her from behind. A strong arm held tightly around her neck, then shoved her through the door and into the house. The briefcase and groceries flew in one direction as Maggie and the cell phone flew in the other.

'Rocco!' She yelled as she flew through the darkness. She was still screaming as her head hit the corner of the end table and her world went black.

★   ★   ★

Maggie awoke to the weight of someone on top of her, tearing her shirt and ripping at her bra. The room was cloaked in darkness and she could hear Prowler growling in the distance. She fought the intruder, scratched at his face, tried to reach for her gun. Her holster was empty. He punched her hard in the face.

'Now it's your turn to listen,' he said.

'Marty?'

'You think you can play house with me and then tell me I'm dismissed?'

'Marty, what are you doing?'

He hit her again.

'You're not calling the shots, I am!'

'Don't be stupid.'

'I was nothing but somebody to service you, you said so. No love songs for you, Maggie. This is what you want, then this is what you get.'

They wrestled on the floor but he had the upper hand. He had caught her off guard and she was still fuzzy from hitting her head. Marty leaned back on his knees and fumbled with his belt. She raised one leg and gave a strong kick. He let out an animal sound as her foot hit its target and got him in the groin. He jumped to his feet, but was buckled forward in pain. Maggie rose and hit him with an upper cut that sent him flying backward. She flipped the light on before he hit the floor with a thud.

She spotted her gun nearly within his reach. He spotted it too and reached toward it. Maggie heard bones snap as she stomped on his hand. He yelled. She reached for her gun as he grabbed her ankle with his undamaged hand. She lost her balance and fell forward onto the floor with a painful thud.

Marty let out a string of profanities as they struggled. He hated her, he'd show her who was boss, she'd get what she was asking for. He called her every filthy name he could think of. The hand she'd stomped on was useless but even one-handed he was strong. But her anger and instincts were stronger.

She escaped from his grip, rose and gave him a hard kick to the side of his head. She grabbed her gun, jumped atop him, and straddled him like a rodeo cowboy.

Maggie cocked the gun and shoved it against the back of his neck. It took every ounce of control she could muster not to pull the trigger. She wanted him dead, but she also wanted him to suffer long and hard for what he'd done.

And for what he'd tried to do.

She knew he was wired wrong but never thought he could be this dangerous. Anger rose like hot lava and bile burned her throat as she spoke.

'Who's calling the shots now, huh, Marty? I told you we weren't right.' She shoved his face into the floor. 'You really need to find yourself a new girlfriend. Somebody more passive. You should know I don't take crap. Not from you. Not from anybody!'

He struggled beneath her and uttered more profanities.

'Don't move or I'll blow your head off.'

Sirens in the distance grew closer and closer. Flashing lights danced across the walls like a psychedelic crazy quilt. Car doors slammed.

'Maggie, you okay in there?'

The door crashed open and there stood Jerry Montana and his sidekick Aaron Iverson, guns pointing around the room then settling their aim at Marty as he continued to struggle beneath her hold. Maggie had never been so happy to see his face.

'Freeze right there,' said the rookie with authority. 'We got you covered and we'll shoot.'

Maggie leaned forward and whispered in Marty's ear like a lover as she pressed the muzzle of her gun harder into the back of his neck. 'You've got three guns on you, Marty. A smarter man might reconsider all that wiggling.'

'Spread your arms out at your sides,' said Jerry Montana. 'And don't move.'

Defeated, he obeyed. Once she felt his muscles relax, Maggie got off him. The rookie cop dragged him to his feet, yanked his arms behind him and clicked on the cuffs.

Jerry looked at her bloody, beaten face and her torn clothes.

'Should we call for a bus? You don't look so good,' he said.

Maggie felt the swelling above her eye and wiped the blood from her mouth.

'No, I'm okay,' she said. 'Just get this creep out of here. Assault and battery on a police officer, unlawful entry, attempted rape, and kidnapping for starters. I'll add more once my head clears.'

'Kidnapping?' Marty yelled, 'You're kidding me.'

'The minute you held me against my will. You're going away for a long time.'

Marty looked at Jerry Montana. 'It's nothing but a little misunderstanding,' he said. 'A lover's spat.'

'Right, this is how he serenades me,' said Maggie.

'Then I guess we can add domestic abuse to the charges.'

Marty released an unearthly growl like a wolf-trapped animal ready to chew off its own leg.

'Jerry,' said Maggie, 'How the hell did you know to come here?'

'Some guy called 911, frantic. He knew your name but not where you were. He gave the dispatcher an earful when he told her you were one of us and we'd better get to you pronto.'

'Thank you both.'

'You betcha,' said Aaron Iverson. 'The caller wanted your address. Damn near chewed the dispatcher's ear off, but she stuck to the rules and didn't budge.'

Jerry Montana pulled out his camera

while Aaron Iverson held the perp. 'We need to photograph the damage, so pose pretty for me, Irish.'

Maggie stood still as he photographed her torn clothes, black eye, and bloody mouth.

The camera flashed and Jerry said, 'Yup, this one'll make a great Miss March for next year's calendar.'

'You're incurable,' Maggie said.

Prowler walked across the room and rubbed against Maggie's leg.

'Did you get the caller's name?'

'Rico something. No, Rocco. Rocco La Crosse,' said the rookie.

Maggie finally remembered they'd been on the cell phone. That hit on the head had knocked it straight out of her. Once again Rocco had entered the picture and this time it probably saved her life. Or Marty's. If Jerry and Aaron hadn't shown up when they did, she might have had no alternative but to shoot Marty. Not that she'd have minded. But that would have involved a long internal investigation. And visits to the shrink. No doubt she'd come out on top, but it would be in her file just the same.

Pain shot through her as she crossed the room and bent down. She groaned as she picked up strewn cans of cat food to the delight of her hungry cat.

'This La Crosse character a friend of yours?' asked Jerry Montana.

'Yeah, I guess you could say he is.'

She looked over at Marty. He was glaring at her, one eye filled with the iciness she'd seen at the café, the other crazy.

'We'll need your statement,' Jerry reminded her.

'I'll give it to you in the morning, Montana. Tonight just get this animal out of my sight and into a cage,' she said. 'I'm tired.'

13

Dwindling Suspects

Maggie assessed the damage as she undressed in front of the bathroom mirror. Bruises were surfacing from head to toe. She turned on the shower. Her body ached and a knot the size of a baseball swelled where her head had hit the end table. Her hands trembled as she downed a handful of aspirin then ran the washcloth painfully across her face. Outside, coyotes yapped at the moon and she heard the snorting and rustling of a family of javelinas as they worked their way down the alley, upending trashcans and rooting out their meals in the darkness. Prowler stood at the bathroom door, stomach full and eyes questioning his mistress.

She dabbed the washcloth gently at her split and swollen lip. 'Ouch! That was some Valentine, wasn't it, boy?'

The cat walked over and squatted in his litter box, then covered his deed.

'My sentiments exactly,' Maggie said. 'But I wish you wouldn't stink up the room when I'm in it.'

She stepped into the shower, welcoming the stream of warm water that caressed her body and washed away the filth of Marty's touch. There was no second guessing. She'd handled him diplomatically, but there was no reasoning with crazy. It took violence to close the book. Too bad she had the bruises and all he had was a very sore groin and a trip to the slammer.

And a few facial scratches.

He deserved more, but that would have to do.

No introspection necessary.

She heard loud banging at the door as she stepped out of the shower. She threw her robe over her damp body. The doorbell rang non-stop as she limped across the living room. Expecting to greet a nosy neighbor, she was surprised to find Rocco La Crosse standing there panting like he'd just run the marathon, perspiration running down his face and into his dark, unkempt beard.

'What, what happened . . . home invasion? What — are you okay? What happened?' He ran the words together, gasping and trying to catch his breath as he leaned against the doorway. He looked disheveled, as though he'd thrown his clothes on as an afterthought. Maggie tightened the sash on her bathrobe, realizing she didn't look any better herself.

'Come on in,' she said. 'You look like you could use a cold one. And so could I.'

When Maggie returned to the living room with the beers, Rocco was sitting on the couch. She handed him one and sat down next to him. As they were uncapping them, she asked: 'How in the world did you find me?'

'You're not listed,' he said, holding up a sheet of crumpled paper. 'I ripped this out of the phone book and worked my way down.' He took a deep draw from the bottle. 'I started banging on doors hoping I'd find a Reardon that knew you — that knew where you lived. I tried to convince them I wasn't a crazy person.' He took a deep breath. 'Congratulations, you're door number five.'

'Thanks for calling 911. I'm beyond grateful. But once you made the call, why go beyond that? Especially for a cop who sees you as a suspect in a murder case.'

'You're the detective, you haven't figured that out yet?'

Maggie didn't know what to say, so she said nothing.

He sat down his beer and straightened out the torn and wrinkled phone book page.

'Who are Michael and Sarah Reardon?' he asked, pointing at the listing.

'My parents,' she said. 'I never got around to changing the listing after they died.'

'Detective Reardon,' he said looking at her bruises.

'We can use first names now, don't you think?'

'Wait here, Maggie.' He rose from the couch and went into the kitchen, returning with ice cubes wrapped in a dish towel and sat down next to her. 'Just hold still,' he said as he pressed the cold cloth against her swollen eye and rested his other hand on her shoulder.

His touch was gentle, his expression reassuring.

'That hurts, but it feels good,' she said.

'So what happened? A home invasion?'

Embarrassed, Maggie lowered her eyes.

'An ex who didn't like the word no.'

He listened as she filled in the details.

'How could he do this?'

'With enthusiasm.'

Rocco pulled her to him and stroked her hair as she leaned her head against his chest.

★ ★ ★

Maggie awoke nestled in the lap of a snoring Rocco with a purring cat draped across her hip. Embarrassed that she'd fallen asleep in his arms she straightened up, freeing his arm that had been folded beneath her and sending Prowler flying to the floor. Rocco opened his eyes and smiled at her, then stretched his arm in front of him and began shaking it.

'It fell numb about two hours ago,' he said, as he shook it back to life.

'Why didn't you just give me an elbow in the ribs?'

'You were sleeping so peacefully.'

Having his arms around her had felt safe and comfortable. Too comfortable. He'd hinted at his feelings, but never made a pass. And Barbara Atwell remained under his roof. He'd offered comfort when she needed it. He was a hard one to figure. Slowly, Maggie stood, every muscle in her body aching and her head throbbing like a scared rabbit's heart. The violence of the previous night came back with every painful movement.

When Rocco La Crosse stood up Maggie noticed the logo on his tee shirt.

'You're a Buddhist?' she said.

'For the most part,' he said, looking down at the yin and yang design on his tee shirt.

'So you're a pacifist then,' she said, relieved. If he was a pacifist it was doubtful he was a murderer.

'That's the part I have a problem with,' he said as he stretched his arms toward the ceiling and yawned. 'The Dalai Lama would be disappointed, but I'd do anything to protect those I care about. So philosophically, yes. You could call me a pacifist, just not in the strictest sense of the word.'

So, who exactly are you protecting? It's right back on the suspect list for you, she thought, disappointed.

But she was attracted to him. Even more so since he'd barged in like a knight in shining armor, determined to protect the very person who held him suspect.

'I've got to brush my teeth,' she said and left the room.

When she came back he was in the kitchen. He'd cleaned up the half empty beer bottles from the night before. And Prowler was eating breakfast.

'Let me fix you something,' he said.

'No. Not a good idea. I've got to get to work. You should go.'

He shrugged. 'Whatever you say.' Then added: 'Barbara's going back to the gallery today and I promised to help Adrian move back there too.'

'You must be disappointed.'

'Why would I be? Those two belong together. It's just too bad it took this tragedy for Barbara to figure it out.'

'And Adrian Velikson might have accelerated things, don't you think?'

'I know you can't trust anyone right now, but I wish you could trust me. Adrian is good at waiting. And she can be jealous. But there's not a violent bone in her body.'

'Your friendship could be clouding your judgment.'

'I trust my feelings. And I trust my feelings for you.'

As much as she wanted to give in to her own, she said, 'We can't go there.'

'We could go for a cup of coffee.'

She walked over to him.

'I can't thank you enough for last night, but it's a bad idea.'

'Do you deny that you're feeling what I am?'

'Rocco,' she said, 'they say if you don't know a horse, look at his track record. Mine is lousy. I'd be a bad bet, believe me.'

'I'm willing to take that gamble.'

'It would be at your peril.' And you might just be a killer, she thought.

Then, as if he was reading her mind, he leaned over and kissed her softly on the forehead. 'I'm one of the good guys,' he said and walked to the door.

There was sadness in his eyes when he turned and looked back at her.

And, without another word, he left.

★ ★ ★

Detective Maggie Reardon went through the motions in a daze. She gave Jerry Montana her statement, sat out the squad room routine impatiently, and refused the suggestion that she go on medical leave. She had a case to solve.

She contacted forensics. Still no results and they were backlogged. She urged them to put her at the top of the list. Instinct told her that the red clay was an important clue in putting the puzzle pieces together.

When she stopped at the mini mart for her coffee she wore her sunglasses and kept her head down. She didn't want the overprotective Carlos to see the bruises or to have to explain. She drove past Viente de Agosto Park, and Crazy Jake and Mouse weren't at their usual spot under the statue. She turned onto Convent Street and pulled up in front of the bright yellow garage door.

'Who is it?' came Jake's voice from inside.

'Detective Reardon,' she said.

'Go away.'

She could hear Mouse whining at him.

'She's a nice lady, Jake. Just stop it.'

Mouse opened the garage door and welcomed her in with a smile.

'Did you catch the guy who killed Armando?'

'We're working on it.'

Maggie looked around the room. A bare mattress lay on the floor, a makeshift sink, and toilet were illegally plumbed into a back corner, and Jake sat in one of two bean bag chairs riddled with rips and duct tape. The sleeping dog was sprawled out on the floor. There was a shelf that held a few books, a couple of bongs, and two of what must have been Armando's

Mexican statues. They were nothing more than cheap tourist crap, just as she'd been told, but she'd have expected to see more of them. Lack of taste not withstanding, they bought them at every reception, so where were they all? She walked over to the shelf and picked one up.

'I can see why you like them,' she said. 'They're charming.'

Jake's eyes were doing the same paranoid dance she'd observed at the park.

'Don't touch that,' he said nervously.

'Calm down, Jake,' said Mouse.

Maggie placed the statue back on the shelf. 'I'm surprised to see so few,' she said. 'I hear you buy a lot of them.'

Mouse hesitated. 'It's just cuz, uh,' she squeaked.

'Let. Me. Talk.' Jake shot her a warning glance as he rose from his bean bag chair.

'Okay, Jake, okay.'

'There ain't no law,' he began. 'So we buy 'em and then we sell 'em for more.' Mouse looked at him with admiration.

'It's called Capitalism,' he smirked.

'Yeah,' she added. 'It gives us a little

more for . . . food.' She looked at Jake for his approval.

Maggie got a nose full of body odor as he walked over and stood in front of her. 'If you got nothin' else, go now,' he said, his rancid breath mixing with the fumes from last week's sweat.

'Thank you for your time,' she said.

When she got to the street, she took a deep breath of fresh air. Even if she could work up a motive for Crazy Jake or Mouse to kill Armando Salazar, she doubted either of the drugged-up pair could muster the necessary motivation.

Maggie took out her notebook and crossed them off her list.

★　★　★

As she drove across town, Rocco La Crosse kept wedging his way into Maggie's thoughts. There was something about this guy, something beyond her attraction to him or her suspicion of him. He'd told her he was one of the good guys. She wondered if he really was. There were so few of them. He was certainly a man who gave generously of his time, as well as of his friendship. He was like a scruffy social worker who appeared to reach out to anyone in need.

He had reached out to her.

And that blasted electricity shot through her every time she was in his presence.

Or thought of him.

She definitely had to put the woman inside her on the back burner.

It was a distraction.

The cop in her came first.

Maggie pulled up in front of the white house and walked through the barren landscape to the front door. On the other side she could hear the cockatoo screeching out his string of profanities and Misty Water's near-whisper admonishing him. There was something about all that white that Maggie found unnerving. It was as though the woman had washed it over herself until she disappeared unnoticed beyond the vale. Behind the *mist.* Exactly what was she hiding?

She rang the doorbell.

And waited.

'Who is it?' Came the whisper from the other side of the door.

'Detective Maggie Reardon.'

Maggie could feel the woman's eyes on her through the peephole in the door.

'I've already told you everything I know.'

'I have a few more questions.'

'I have no answers. Please go away.'

'You have one answer.'

Silence.

'What is your name?'

'My name is Misty Waters.' Tension strained her voice. 'Misty. Waters.'

'There is no Misty Waters,' said Maggie. 'What is your name?'

Maggie didn't know what to make of the mournful sobs beyond the door.

'Your name.'

'M-mmm-misty.'

'Name!'

'Leave me alone!' It was the first time she had heard her raise her voice.

'Who are you?'

Maggie Reardon detected genuine terror in the artist's voice as she replied.

'Wendy Masterson,' she screamed.

'Now go away and leave me alone!'

Misty Waters. Wendy Masterson. M.W., W.M. People frequently kept their own initials when they came up with an alias. Maybe that made the lie easier to remember. But why would this apparently passive person need an alias?

'What are you hiding?' she asked.

But there was no answer.

* * *

Maggie Reardon sat in front of the computer screen at her desk, searching.

Misty Waters, Wendy Masterson.

Like her previous search the name Misty Waters got no hits.

She had entered Wendy Masterson in the data base and found no criminal record. For some reason that didn't surprise her. But the woman was definitely hiding something.

And Detective Maggie Reardon was determined to find out what.

She Googled Wendy Masterson into her laptop and waited.

The phone at her desk rang and she

picked up. It was Forensics.

'We have some information,' said the voice at the other end. 'Not all of it, but some of the red clay from the Armando Salazar crime scene is a perfect match to the piece of pottery you gave us. And it matches the shards from the victim's skull.'

So, Belinda Blume's Gaia sculpture was the murder weapon, just as she'd suspected.

'Thank you for verifying my suspicions.'

'A cop's gut instinct is rarely wrong, Detective. But it never hurts to have a little science to back it up.'

'Too much television,' Maggie said. 'Juries today expect forensics to come into play. And it usually does. The advances in science have been nothing short of miraculous. The down side is that jurors tend to dismiss common sense when DNA and forensics don't play into things. They always see it on their crime dramas and they expect it. We can give them a string of circumstantial evidence that could form no other conclusion but guilt, but they still want that fingerprint.'

'Speaking of which,' the voice at the other end replied, 'we're trying to pull a print from the largest shard. I'll give you a call as soon as we have something.'

'Thanks.'

'I'm sorry we took so long, Detective Reardon, but the lab is really backed up right now. And I have one more bit of news for you.'

'Yes?'

'That powder on the clay bits you brought in? It was cocaine.'

'Interesting. That gives me something new to work with,' Maggie said. 'Thanks again and I'll be waiting to hear from you on the prints. Thanks for a great job.'

Did cocaine fit into the murder scenario or was it just the residue from a bunch of bohemians having their fun? Even Mary Rose liked to get a little high with her tea, so a little white powder at the gallery should come as no surprise.

She hung up the phone and focused on the computer screen.

There were several hits on the name Wendy Masterson and Maggie began reading through them and jotting down notes.

'Oh, my god,' she said aloud.

She fished through her desk drawer, retrieved a stack of business cards and shuffled through them until she found the right one.

Detective Maggie Reardon picked up the phone.

14

The Darkest Secrets

It was early afternoon when the three friends marched single file through the shadows of the side yard at The Mosaic Gallery. Rocco La Crosse led the way as they passed the palo verde trees and up the steps to the back apartment. He climbed the stairs carrying a large cardboard box, and Barbara Atwell and Adrian Velikson followed behind him. When they reached the top, Rocco sat his box on the landing and Barbara and Adrian sat their smaller boxes on top of his. Barbara reached into her purse and pulled out her key. She opened the door and walked inside, holding the door open for them.

'Welcome home,' Rocco said.

'It feels good,' said Barbara.

'And it feels right,' said Adrian.

They carried in Adrian's three boxes

and sat them on the floor.

Adrian collapsed on the couch as Barbara looked around the room.

'I can hardly believe I'm back,' she said.

'That's the easiest move I've ever made,' said Rocco. 'You're definitely not a pack rat, Adrian. I can't believe you fit everything from your apartment into three boxes.'

'I believe in traveling light,' she said. 'It simplifies life.'

'I'll be right back,' Rocco said to Barbara. 'I still need to bring up your clothes and stuff.'

'I don't know about you two, but I've worked up an appetite,' said Adrian. 'I think I'll call out for a pizza.'

'I've got some soda in the fridge.'

Adrian reached for the phone.

Rocco whistled as he skipped down the stairs and out to his van. It struck him as funny that Adrian could carry her life in three boxes and Barbara needed that much just for a few days at his house. It reminded him of the old George Carlin routine about 'stuff.' Adrian had the right idea. Rocco's mind wandered. His favorite spendthrift relative had so much stuff he had to rent two storage units just to have room for it all. The guy would probably go through his entire inheritance never having a clue where it all went. He was a good example of why, no matter how hard the well-intentioned might be, there could never be financial equality. Give two people the exact same amount of money and within twenty-four hours one would be poorer and the other would have invested and started to build up the original amount. Rocco was generous with his charitable contributions but he chose them thoughtfully. He believed strongly in giving people a hand up rather than a handout. He had a big house although he could afford a bigger one. He had all the room he needed, and about the only stuff he let collect there was the dust on the top of his books.

His books were his guilty pleasure.

He slammed the van door shut and headed back up the stairs, Barbara's belongings in hand.

Calypso was sifting through overflowing piles of torn, colorful paper at the dining room table. Each piece would eventually work its way into a collage or onto a decorated box. She tossed the warm colors into one pile, the cools in another, the bits of broken jewelry into a bucket that sat on the floor.

Middle Eastern music played softly from the stereo.

The doorbell rang, startling her.

And interrupting her focus, what there was of it.

'Detective Reardon here.'

It had skipped Calypso's mind that they'd made an appointment.

'Enter,' she said, 'the door's open.' Calypso ran over to the couch and tossed a pile of laundry onto the floor to give the detective a place to sit. She tossed a stack of magazines and unopened mail onto the coffee table and sat down.

Maggie looked around the room. Once again, there was that faint aroma of stale marijuana smoke, this time mixed with the smell of French fries. A crumpled bag from a local fast food joint sat among the clutter on the coffee table. There were piles of trash everywhere, but there was organization in the chaos, things separated into some weird theme, mostly by color. There were piles of paper and buckets of broken jewelry. Plastic flowers lay in a heap in a corner. Maggie's eyes settled on a wall filled with artwork. Collages like she'd seen at the gallery. Happy, optimistic splashes of color perfectly put together. The woman created treasure from trash. But oh, the trash. She wondered how the artist named Calypso was able to make heads or tails of it all.

She returned her attention to Calypso who sat there with disheveled orange hair, looking like an unmade bed in a sea of junk jewelry.

'I heard about Armando Salazar,' she said. 'Is that why you're here?'

'I'm speaking with everyone who was at the gallery that night.'

'What do you want to know?'

'How close were you?'

'What do you mean by close?'

'Would you have considered him a friend?'

'He wasn't anything but the guy who served the drinks.'

Calypso leaned forward and started shuffling through a stack of papers. She rose, grabbed a few pieces, and flitted over to the dining room table where she separated them into more piles.

'I'm sorry, did you ask me something?' she said, reentering the room.

Maggie flipped through her notepad and looked up.

'You had no interest in him?'

'Okay, I'm busted,' she said with a shrug. 'I found him attractive.'

Once again, Calypso became distracted and started swaying to the music.

'Would you say the attraction was mutual?' Maggie remembered Mary Rose's comment about her friend being upset at her flirtations being rejected by Armando.

Calypso stopped moving, her expression unreadable. She reached over and picked up a length of gauzy fabric that was draped over a chair. 'I also dance at The Oasis,' she said, twirling the fabric. 'I'm their star. This would make a great costume, don't you think?'

'About Armando,' Maggie began.

'He was married to a woman twice his age and he couldn't see me?' Calypso swayed to the music and managed to gracefully sidestep the clutter strewn across the floor. Her disheveled appearance made her comical. Maggie wondered if she cleaned up any better when she had to perform. 'Look at me,' she said as she danced across the room then stood before the detective. 'I'm irresistible when I dance.'

'So, your opinion of Armando Salazar?'

'He was arrogant and he was uppity.' she said, 'and he was obviously blind.'

★ ★ ★

Spring from Vivaldi's *Four Seasons* whispered softly from the stereo speakers, matching the relaxed mood of the room.

'It's good seeing the two of you here together again,' said Rocco, lifting his slice of pizza and taking a bite. 'Things have come full circle.'

'Sometimes I think you know us better than we know ourselves,' said Barbara.

'Speak for yourself,' said Adrian with a satisfied smile. 'I've always known that we were meant to be like this.'

'And you were always right,' said Barbara, reaching her arm across the other woman's shoulders. 'If I'd listened to you none of this would ever have happened.'

'It's time to focus on the positive and embrace the good,' Rocco said.

Barbara hesitated, then said, 'I just wish they'd find out who it was.'

'Detective Reardon's doing her job,' he said. 'If anybody can figure out who killed Armando, It's Maggie.'

'Maggie?' teased Adrian, 'so you two are on a first name basis now?'

'More or less,' he said, embarrassed.

'Why, Rocco La Crosse,' said Adrian. 'I think you have a crush on her.'

'Could be.'

'You look like the proverbial cat who ate the canary,' Barbara said.

'Let me clean up this mess,' he said, changing the subject and gathering their empty plates. 'Thanks for lunch, Adrian,' he said from the kitchen. 'I didn't realize how hungry I was.'

'Hey, it's the least I could do to thank you.'

'No thanks required,' he said. 'If you don't need me for anything else I'm going to hit the road. There's a project at home that's calling my name.'

He picked up the empty pizza box and headed for the door.

'I'll drop this in the bin downstairs,' he said.

As he closed the door behind him he heard Barbara say, 'Adrian, there's something we need to talk about.'

★　★　★

When Maggie walked into the mini-mart, Carlos was busy with customers. She readjusted her sunglasses and headed for the back to get a burrito. She'd eat on the run as she headed to the other side of town to question the next person on her list. She held the hot burrito in her hand and walked down one of the aisles for chips, filled a cup with cola, snapped on the lid and inserted a straw. The front door dinged as customers left one by one until she was the only person left.

'This morning you did no fool me,' Carlos called out her.

'What?' she asked as she walked up and placed her food on the counter.

'You think sunglasses hide the bruises on your cheek? Or your swollen lip?'

'You didn't say anything.'

'I could see you didn't want to talk.'

Maggie removed her shades, exposing her black eye.

'I'd tell you I ran into a door but I doubt you'd believe me.'

'Oh Miss Maggie, it looks like one of the crooks got the best of you.'

'You should see the other guy,' she said.

'That's not funny. I tell you many times your job is too dangerous.'

'It didn't happen on the job. And my job's no more dangerous than you working here all alone.'

He shrugged.

'You want to tell *papacita* what happened?'

She filled him in on the events of the previous night.

'Maggie, Maggie. If I had your gun I'd gladly shoot him myself. What kind of *loco* person could this be?'

'A man who doesn't like no for an answer.'

'He is no man, he is a coward.'

'Carlos, that was yesterday. I've put it behind me.'

'And tell me, Miss Maggie. Every time you look in the mirror and see what this bad man did to you, can you put it behind you then?'

'The bruises will fade, Carlos.' And I don't believe in lugging around emotional scars, she thought to herself. Life's got enough checked baggage without adding a carry-on.

* * *

Paloma Blanca, the jewelry artist, sat across from Maggie as she reeled off the standard questions. The woman was

247

young, she was beautiful, and she knew it. Her name was the polar opposite of her appearance. In Spanish, Paloma Blanca means white dove. Paloma had jet black hair and eyes as dark as a Madrid midnight against perfect alabaster skin. She was stunning. She was as striking in her dark Latin beauty as Barbara Atwell was in her blonde sophistication. Mr. Armando Salazar had temptation all around him and apparently had his pick, although he showed no favoritism and had opted for them all.

Except for Calypso.

Even Armando had some standards.

The two women played question and answer, Paloma's responses short and abrupt with no hesitations.

'Armando Salazar was planning on seeing you that night,' Maggie said.

'We hook up from time to time, yes. He never showed up so I went out.'

'Hook up?'

'For sex.'

'So you didn't wait for him?'

'I don't wait for anyone, Detective Reardon. And I wasn't about to wait for him. I went out nightclubbing. I had no idea what had happened, but believe me I'd have gone dancing anyway. I believe in devouring life, not waiting on a bus bench for it to find me.'

'So you two weren't serious?'

'I wasn't. And Armando wasn't serious about anything. It was recreational sex, nothing more.'

'And there was nothing about this relationship that bothered you?'

'It was strictly for fun. I'm young and I'm single and I have every intention of partying until my bones get too brittle to dance the salsa.'

'So his being married wasn't a problem?'

'Armando might have been married, but I'm not.'

'I see.'

'If anybody had an issue regarding his marital status it should have been his wife.'

'Did she know?'

'Oh, she knew. She might not have known who, where, or when, but she knew who she married.'

'And you don't think it concerned her?'

'I think Barbara Atwell took pride in the fact that he always came back. He was younger, you know, by several years. I don't mean that in a catty way, but he was her trophy. And he was always back in her bed before the rooster crowed, so I doubt she complained.'

The compromises people made. Even if these people enjoyed their carefree Bohemian lifestyle, Maggie couldn't wrap her head around it. If she'd had a husband who carried on, she'd drop him in a heartbeat. In her book being alone was preferable to being with the wrong person. She saw Barbara Atwell as proof that you don't have to be stupid to be a fool.

'Thank you for your time, Miss Blanca. I appreciate your cooperation.'

'Find the person who did this,' she said. 'For Barbara's sake. Despite what you might think Detective Reardon, I consider Barbara my friend.'

★   ★   ★

'I asked that you not bother me.' Misty Waters voice was barely audible as she whispered through the door. 'Please, please go away.'

'I'm not here as a cop, Misty. I'm here to help.'

'I don't need your help. I don't want it.'

'Please listen. I know what happened to you and I understand. I know what you're hiding from.'

Silence.

'I can help you.'

There was a long pause and then, one by one, Maggie Reardon heard the locks being unbolted. The door opened a crack and Misty peered out.

'You can't help something that's already done.'

Maggie pulled off her sunglasses and showed Misty her bruised and battered face. 'I have some small idea of what you've been through.'

'Come in.'

The two women sat on the white couch in the whiter room, Maggie wearing the physical bruises from her encounter with Marty, and Misty wearing the emotional scars from an attack far more brutal than the one Maggie had endured. They sat in silence for a long time, except for the occasional expletive blurted out by the white cockatoo in his cage.

'I read the newspaper reports and I read the court transcripts and I understand what you've gone through.'

'He was a neighbor,' she said. 'He said he wanted to borrow a mixing bowl, so I thought nothing of asking him in.'

'Go on.'

'Don't tell anyone my name is Wendy Masterson,' she said, panic straining her voice. 'He could find me.'

'It's between us. I promise.'

'It was my fault,' she continued. 'Not that he raped me, but . . . after he left I ran to the bathtub and I scrubbed and scrubbed his filth off of me until my flesh was bleeding. I wasn't thinking of the rape kit or the evidence or anything like that. I just wanted to feel clean again.'

Maggie reached over and took her hand.

'The police did their job, Detective Reardon. They caught him. But the court

. . . I mean, it was my fault that it was just his word against mine, I'd washed away the evidence. But the defense attorney . . . ' Tears were running down her face. 'He made horrible innuendos. Like why I'd asked him in and how I liked it rough and — '

'The usual,' Maggie said. 'The courts still have a lot of catching up to do. A woman is raped in this country every two and a half minutes. The statistics are staggering, yet when a woman finds the courage to face her attacker she's the one put on trial. I know: I've seen it too many times.'

'When they said not guilty he looked right at me. That sick smile of his told me he was coming back for more. I didn't even go home. I cleaned out my bank account and went straight to the airport and got a ticket on the next plane out. I didn't care where to.'

'You've allowed this monster to own your life, Misty.'

'He could find me, I know he could.'

'No, he can't. I did some research. Your attacker was linked to the rape and murder of three women outside Hartford. He hanged himself while he was awaiting trial. He's dead, Misty. He'll never hurt anyone again. He'll never hurt you.'

She started crying, loud and mournful sobs, gasping until she couldn't breathe. Detective Maggie Reardon held the broken woman close to her and let her cry tears that were long overdue. She wept for a long time, until there were no more tears left to cry.

'It's time you took your life back,' said Maggie.

'I don't know how. I don't think I can.'

Maggie took the business card from her pocket and handed it to her.

'I spoke to this woman and she will show you how. She works for the Center Against Sexual Assault, and she'll see you receive all the counseling you need.'

'I don't understand why you're helping me.'

'Because I care. You're a free woman now, Misty Waters. You're free to be whomever you choose to be, be it Misty Waters or Wendy Masterson or someone else entirely. You own you.'

Misty stared at the card in her hand.

'And you might consider getting rid of that bird.'

15

To the Slaughter

The temperatures dropped as scattered clouds blocked the late afternoon sun. Maggie Reardon sat at her desk finishing up the day's paperwork. She held hope that Misty Waters would call the number on the card. The woman's eyes held less fear. And there was a faint glimmer of, what was it, hope? Despite not having yet solved the Armando Salazar murder, Maggie had accomplished something important. Something good. She leaned back in her chair, satisfied.

'Hey, Irish.'

'Montana.'

'Man, you're face looks like raw hamburger,' he said, eyeing her bruises.

'You come to gloat?'

'No, actually I'm here to call a truce.'

'A truce?'

'We're fighting on the same team, Maggie.

I want to apologize for giving you a hard time. I didn't really mean anything by it.'

'It sounds like a bit of Aaron Iverson is rubbing off on you.'

He shrugged.

'I'm willing to put it behind me if you are,' she said.

'Friends, then?'

'Let's not go that far, not yet anyway.'

'That's a start.'

★ ★ ★

Prowler sat on Maggie Reardon's lap while she ate a donut and watched the early morning news. The cat licked up the powdered sugar that sifted onto her bathrobe. The heat had dropped ten degrees and there was a vague reference to rain in the forecast. It wasn't carved in stone, the weather never was, but it was a step in the right direction.

'This is a tough one,' she said to the cat. 'I thought Misty Waters was hiding something, but she was hiding *from* something. I doubt that she's our perp. The two drugged-up hippies don't have a motive.'

Prowler meowed.

'I know, I could've busted them for drug paraphernalia and I suppose I could have even busted Mary Rose, but why bother? No harm, no foul, really. Jake and Mouse have enough problems and Mary Rose, well, I like her. So would you. You might even like her cat.'

Prowler settled into her lap.

'Calypso is too much of a scatterbrain,' she rambled on out loud, 'although it wouldn't be impossible. So that leaves Belinda Blume, Paloma Blanca, and maybe Rocco La Crosse.' There's those little butterflies again, she thought, dismissing them. 'If Barbara Atwell had a motive, I can't figure it. Adrian Velikson definitely had a motive. The oldest in the book. And then there's always the unknown. The random element. But we're narrowing things down.'

Maggie jumped when the cell phone rang. She reached over to the side table and picked up.

It was Forensics.

'Reardon here.'

'I've got some results for you, Detective

Reardon. Toxicology came back. Armando Salazar had traces of cocaine in his system and his blood alcohol was 0.10, so he was definitely flying high. And we were able to pull a few partials from the largest clay shard.'

'That's great,' she said. The break she'd been waiting for. The prints wouldn't necessarily be that of the killer, but it was more likely than not. They'd only had a few pieces of clay to work with but they were, after all, fragments from the murder weapon.

The other end of the phone was silent.

'Yes?' Maggie said.

'We got matches on both prints.'

Maggie pushed the cat off her lap. She reached over for her notepad and pen and began writing.

Two suspects, two motives.

One dead body.

* * *

'I'll get it,' Barbara Atwell said to Adrian. 'It's probably another nosy neighbor. That yellow tape really brought the vultures out to feed.' When she answered the door she was surprised to see the detective standing there.

'I hope this visit means you've caught my Armando's killer,' she said as she ushered Maggie inside. 'I'll never rest until he's caught.'

'We're close,' Maggie said, observing the exchange of glances between Barbara and Adrian.

'A cup of coffee?' Adrian offered.

'I could use one, thanks,' she said. 'Black.'

Adrian retreated to the kitchen and came back with a steaming mug, hands trembling as she handed it to the detective. Maggie pretended she hadn't noticed, and let the hot liquid burn across her tongue and down her throat, then leaned back in her chair.

'We've lifted a few prints from the murder weapon. Or what was left of it,' she said.

Again the two women exchanged glances.

'The murder weapon?' asked Barbara.

'We can go into that later. Adrian,

would you mind coming down to headquarters with me? I'd like to ask you a few more questions.'

'Detective Reardon! Are you arresting her?' Asked Barbara, alarm in her voice. 'You can't possibly — '

'Barbara, be quiet, I can handle this.'

'No, I'm not arresting her. There's just a few things we need to clear up.'

'And if she chooses not to go?'

'I can get a warrant, come back, cuff her, and take her anyway.'

'Barb, I told you I can handle this.' She shot a look at her that said *shut up*.

The two women definitely knew something.

'I'd appreciate your cooperation, Adrian. We can do this the easy way or we can do it the hard way.'

Adrian Velikson looked down at the floor and ran her hands through her short hair. Barbara leaned over and put her arms around her. 'You don't have to do this,' she said. 'Just tell her no.'

Adrian pulled away from her and stood up.

'I'm ready to cooperate with you any

way I can,' she said, holding out her tattooed arms. 'Do you need to cuff me?'

'You've been watching too much television. We're just going to talk.'

'Let's go then.'

'I want to come along.'

'Stay here, Barbara. I'll be right back.'

Barbara Atwell watched from the window and when the car pulled away, she retrieved her key to the gallery and walked down the stairs. Memories of Armando drenched in his own blood flooded over her as she entered the room.

Life would never be the same.

She sat at her desk and fished through the file drawer, then retrieved a stack of papers. She sorted through them and settled on the last page. She rose and walked through the rooms of The Mosaic Gallery, looking at the walls, the paintings, at a lifetime of work. She walked back to her desk and sat down. She picked up her pen, wrote something on the document, and carried it with her as she walked back up the stairs.

* * *

Detective Maggie Reardon walked Adrian Velikson down the long hallway at the police station. Jerry Montana spotted her and rushed up, pulling her aside.

'What is it, Montana? If you haven't noticed, I'm a little busy right now.'

'I was just wondering,' he whispered, 'if you need somebody to help you play good cop/bad cop.'

'I've got it under control,' she said, 'but thanks. I'll buzz you if it comes to that.'

'I'm really good at playing bad cop.' He smiled, and walked away.

She led Adrian through the door, shutting it behind them.

Detective Maggie Reardon and Adrian Velikson sat across the table from each other in the interrogation room. Maggie turned on the tape player to record their conversation. She looked up at the corner of the ceiling to double-check that the video camera had been activated. Its red light winked back at her. Adrian stared at her hands then looked around the room.

'I've asked some of these questions before, but I'd like to go over them again. Why don't we start with your relationship with Barbara Atwell.'

'What do you want to know?'

'What do you want to tell me?'

'You know everything, detective. We're friends. We're soul mates.'

'And her marriage to Armando?'

'I learned to accept it.'

'The night of the reception, what time did you leave?'

'When it closed, I've already told you.'

'And you went straight home?'

'Yes.'

'Can anyone verify that?'

'Not unless you want to count the gang-wannabees that hang out in front of my apartment building. I doubt you'd consider them credible witnesses.'

'And the last time you saw Armando?'

'When I found him dead. Detective, you should be looking for someone intent on robbing the gallery. It's the only thing that makes sense.'

'It might if something had been stolen.'

'The Gaia statue was stolen,' she said.

'Before we continue I need to inform you that you have the right to an attorney,' Maggie said and reeled off the

Miranda Rights to the woman across from her. 'Do you understand?'

'Perfectly.'

'And you're willing to continue?'

'Yes.'

'I think you know who the murderer was.'

Adrian fidgeted, shifted her weight, looked around the room to avoid eye contact with Maggie. Then she straightened up in her chair.

'I killed him,' she said.

That wasn't the response Maggie had expected. Not yet anyway. The tough little woman folded like she'd been under water torture, catching Maggie by surprise.

'Because?' she asked.

'I was tired of sharing, you can understand that. He was in the way. Is that all?' Her voice was controlled, her demeanor calm.

This was easy. Maybe too easy.

'The murder weapon?'

'What?'

'What did you use to kill him?'

'I hit him over the head. Hard.'

'With what?'

'I can't remember,' she said. 'It all happened so fast.'

'We have your prints on the murder weapon,' Maggie said.

'Well, I just told you I killed him, didn't I?'

'But you can't remember with what?'

'I guess you'll have to refresh my memory. Better yet, why don't you just book me and get this over with? I've held this inside long enough. I've confessed and I'm ready to accept my punishment. That's all you need.' Then she added: 'I'm tired of talking to you, detective.'

'Just one more question,' Maggie said.

There was a knock on the interrogation room door.

'Just a minute,' Maggie said as she rose and crossed the room.

When she opened the door Jerry Montana stood there.

'Could you come out here for a minute?' he asked.

'I hope this is important.'

'Oh, it's interesting,' he said with his usual smirk.

'Stay put, Adrian,' she said. 'I'll be right back.'

'Do I look like I'm going anywhere?' she said, looking up at the surveillance camera.

Maggie stepped into the hallway, closing the door behind her.

'What is it, Jerry?'

'We've got a real looker up at the front desk. Tall, pretty blonde says she needs to talk to you. Name's Barbara Atwell. That's your widow from the gallery, isn't it?'

Maggie nodded.

'Anyway, she's all frantic and says it's important. I told her you were busy, but — '

Detective Reardon headed for the front desk and Jerry followed, not wanting to miss any of the action. Heck, maybe he could end up consoling the grieving widow, who knows?

'Barbara, I'm busy right now,' Maggie said to her. 'If you could wait here, I'll get to you shortly.'

'This can't wait, detective.'

'Why?'

'I need to see Adrian. And I have something I need to tell you.'

'Let's go then, but this had better be important.'

Maggie motioned Jerry Montana to back off and give her some space. He watched the two as they walked down the hall to the interrogation room. Adrian turned and rose from her chair as Barbara rushed through the door and embraced her.

'You shouldn't have come,' Adrian said.

'Enough is enough.'

'But I've already told her what happened.' She held Barbara firmly by the shoulders and looked into her eyes. 'I already confessed, so please. Just. Go. Home.'

'You two ladies need to sit down,' said Maggie as she pulled up a chair for Barbara. 'You want to tell me what's going on?'

The two of them sat.

'Just shut up,' said Adrian to Barbara. 'It's done.'

'No, it's not. I can't let you do this!'

'I already told her that I killed him.'

'Detective Reardon,' Barbara said over Adrian's protests, 'I killed Armando. It was me.'

Was Barbara protecting Adrian or was it the other way around? Maggie asked her the one question that Adrian seemed unable to answer.

'What was the murder weapon?'

'The Gaia statue,' she said matter-of-factly.

'Then why do you think we found Adrian's prints on it?'

Barbara thought hard.

'I remember,' she said. 'Belinda brought in the statue and sat it on the pedestal. I remember Adrian going over and lifting it, commenting on how beautiful it was. And how heavy. I'm sure that's how her prints got there. As sure as I am that several other people touched it during the evening. It got a lot of attention.'

It made sense. The only other prints they were able to pull belonged to the artist, Belinda Blume. There were likely even more prints from more people, but a few small pieces were all forensics had to work with. And Barbara knew it was the murder weapon. So far, Barbara's answers made more sense than Adrian's, but Maggie needed more. Barbara waived her Miranda Rights and chose to continue.

'Don't do this,' Adrian said.

'I love you Adrian, it's what I have to do.'

'I'm listening,' Maggie said. 'Why don't you start from the beginning.'

★ ★ ★

The last of the customers left the gallery and Barbara Atwell locked the door. Armando walked over and gave her a kiss.

'I think it went well,' he said as they walked into the far room. 'I sold many tonight.'

'Why don't we go upstairs and catch up with the other thing?' she suggested.

'Mañana, my love, tonight I am going out for awhile. And you need your sleep.'

'I'm tired of you always leaving me. Why can't you stay home and give me what you're giving every other female in this town?'

'I thought we had an understanding. Don't demean yourself.'

'I'm tired of understanding.'

Armando walked over to the bar and emptied the remainder of a bottle of champagne into a glass. He drained the glass, set it down hard and looked at his watch.

'Not now. This will wait until morning.'

'No, it won't wait,' she said, moving towards him.

He shoved her.

'We need to talk now,' she demanded.

He shoved her harder and she reeled backwards and into the shelf that held his statues. Several of them fell and broke at her feet.

'You foolish gringa! Look what you have done.'

Barbara looked down at the broken figurines, bent over and lifted one, ready to apologize. White powder poured out of the broken statue and onto the floor. Armando turned as white as the powder.

'What is this?' She dampened her finger and ran it along the inside of the piece.

271

'What it is, is no your business,' he said.

She touched her finger to her tongue and tasted it.

'How could you do this to me! How could you do this to the gallery?'

'Is no your business,' he repeated.

'Smuggling cocaine in those stupid little statues is none of my business? No wonder they sell! You could ruin me!'

Armando shoved her again, harder this time. Barbara had never been so angry as when he came at her again, his fist raised. She turned and picked up the Gaia statue and held it over her head.

'Don't come any closer. I'm warning you.'

'You wouldn't dare,' he said, laughing as he turned away.

★ ★ ★

'I didn't mean to kill him,' Barbara said. 'I worked my whole life to build up The Mosaic Gallery and he was going to ruin everything. I couldn't let that happen. I never wanted him dead, but he was. So I swept up and threw things into the neighbor's trash bin.'

Adrian took her hand.

'You should have let me take the blame,' she said.

'You could be charged with withholding information,' said Maggie to Adrian.

'She didn't know until yesterday.'

'And how long has Rocco La Crosse known?'

'He doesn't know.'

'Your best friend? I find that hard to believe.'

'I couldn't put him in that position.'

'Being?'

'Making the choice between supporting his friend or doing the right thing.'

Maggie looked at the two women. Barbara reached into her purse, pulled out some papers, and handed them to Adrian.

'What are these?' Adrian asked.

'The gallery is yours now. Yours and Rocco's.'

'But . . . '

'Don't argue. I want you to have it.'

Maggie couldn't help but feel touched.

It wasn't often she saw such deep love and dedication.

'I'm not a lawyer and I can't give legal advice,' said Maggie, 'but this wasn't First Degree Murder. Not by a long shot. Call it a crime of passion or even stretch it to self-defense. Get a good enough lawyer and he can probably plea it down from there.'

'I'll do whatever it takes,' said Adrian.

And Maggie knew she would.

★ ★ ★

Drops of rain fell on the blacktop as Detective Reardon walked across the parking lot to her car. She pulled her cell phone from her pocket and punched in the number.

'Hello Rocco,' she said. 'This is Maggie.' She raised her head and let the welcome rain wash against her face. 'If you're still interested, I'm ready for that cup of coffee.'

THE END